THOSE
WHO
DISAPPEARED

OTHER TITLES BY KEVIN WIGNALL

Individual Works

People Die

Among the Dead

Who is Conrad Hirst?

The Hunter's Prayer

Dark Flag

A Death in Sweden

The Traitor's Story

A Fragile Thing

To Die in Vienna

When We Were Lost

The Names of the Dead

Short Stories

"The Window"

"Retrospective"

"A Death"

"Hal Checks Out"

KEVIN WIGNALL

THOSE WHO DISAPPEARED

THOMAS & MERCER

Text copyright © 2021 by Kevin Wignall
All rights reserved.

Published by Thomas & Mercer, Seattle

www.apub.com

Amazon, the Amazon logo, and Thomas & Mercer are trademarks of Amazon.com, Inc., or its affiliates.

ISBN-13: 9781542023474
ISBN-10: 1542023475

Cover design by @blacksheep-uk.com

Printed in the United States of America

THOSE
WHO
DISAPPEARED

Prologue

There was peace in the mountains, but it was a brittle peace. The hollowness in the air and the pristine expanse of the weekend's heavy snowfall might have promised something different in January, but late April was too late and this felt like a dangerous place to be now.

For Brett, that was part of the appeal. Since leaving the *pension*, he hadn't seen another person. The other hikers staying there had heeded the official warnings or just shied away from the extra effort of climbing through a few feet of fresh snow.

It was hard work, there was no question of that, and the constant dripping of water from the pine trees and the insistent gabbling of fast-running streams here and there within the forest were evidence enough that the warnings weren't empty threats. This was a winter landscape, but it was no longer winter and its instability was everywhere around him, even in the air itself, which was not quite cold enough.

Brett pressed on, and when he cleared the tree line he got the first glimpse of what he'd come for. The Handeck Glacier stretched out ahead of him to the left, a sweeping frozen river of ripples and eddies filling the valley. He kept climbing, inching closer, and couldn't take his eyes off it, paying almost no attention now to the surrounding peaks and the fragile glistening snowfields. He kept climbing until the river of ice was almost within touching distance below him.

He'd expected the glacier to hum and crackle as he got closer, for its incremental movement to bristle through the clear air, but when he stopped walking there was no sound at all, not even wind or birdsong or the hum of distant cars or trains far down in the valley. He stood there looking out across the expanse of ice, smiling, even laughing a little, silently, overwhelmed by the immensity of it, and by the fact that he was alone to see it, a private viewing.

The sound, when it came, was so slight as to barely register. It was somewhere far above and behind him, a noise like canvas tearing, or like distant firecrackers that were damp and failing to ignite properly. He turned, curious rather than alarmed, as a deceptively gentle thunder rippled through the valley, and he still couldn't see anything moving on the slopes above, but when the ground began to tremble beneath him, he finally understood what was happening.

An avalanche. He felt his muscles flood with adrenaline, his stomach tight and hollow, a screaming moment of indecision, panic disabling him.

He looked back along the path toward the distant forest, far below him now. But there was no feature he could see to offer protection, nothing above or ahead of him either. Without even thinking, he scrambled directly downhill, off the path, aiming for one of the small bluffs that punctuated the lower side of the valley.

Even as he reached it and pushed himself hard against the rock face, the ground was thrumming beneath him and the air had turned white. The wall of snow roared past and engulfed him with a deafening, pummeling force that sucked the breath out of his lungs. He pushed harder against the rock and then in an instant the rock was gone from him.

Brett felt himself inside the void, and time slowed so that he had plenty of opportunity to think about landing before his body actually made contact. As soon as he felt the first crunching impact, he tried to move his arms and legs, determined not to be buried and suffocated, but he was still careering downward and his arms were yanked behind him as he tumbled on into the thundering abyss.

The noise and violence stopped so suddenly that it took him unawares, and with another moment of panic he once again flailed his arms and legs before realizing he was only partially submerged. The bluff had apparently sheltered him just long enough, and apart from a searing pain in his shoulder and a ringing in his ears, he seemed unharmed.

The cloud of snow fell away and he saw that he'd descended a hundred feet or more, and was now perched immediately above the near side of the glacier. For a moment there was silence again, but then something small and hard hit the back of his head as a cascade of stones showered down. He heard a whistling sound and saw a boulder fly past a couple of feet away and crash down into the edge of the glacier.

He flattened himself back into the snow, turning face down, pressing hard, and he lay like that for what felt like minutes, until he was convinced nothing else was coming down the mountain. When he did move, it was with a delayed panic, jumping up, struggling to get his balance, looking urgently from side to side. Finally he felt safe enough for self-recrimination, cursing himself for having ignored the warnings, for almost becoming one of those foolish casualties for whom the public would have no sympathy.

He brushed the snow from his body, wincing with the pain in his shoulder the whole time. He looked back up the slope, searching for the best route to regain the path, or what was left of the path. With that thought he turned and looked where the boulder had shattered into the side of the glacier, ripping off a chunk of ice and exposing the grainy interior.

Brett stared at it for a few seconds, puzzled by the dark patterns within the freshly calved ice. He took out his phone, opened the camera—his hands still trembling—and zoomed in. It still wasn't clear and yet, from here at least, it looked . . .

He put the phone back in his pocket and picked his way carefully down the newly made slope—sinking up to his knees with each step, stumbling but never falling again—until he was close enough to be sure. A small patch of red material protruded from the wall of ice, and beyond it, a shadowy presence that was unmistakable.

Brett couldn't see the features, couldn't see any details at all, and yet there was no doubt it was a man in there. Who knew how long he'd been there or who he was. A short time before, Brett had come so close to losing his own life, a fraction of time or space away, and now he was faced with the reality of life and death in these mountains.

The stillness was eerie now, so profound that his senses sought to fill the vacuum. The glacier sounded as if it were whispering, murmuring, and a couple of times Brett jumped and looked around, thinking someone had approached behind him.

He jumped a third time when he turned back and thought the body had shifted within the ice, but it was only the light hitting the glacier at a different angle. The man entombed there was no threat to anyone.

Brett reached for his phone again, his hands trembling even more, his heartbeat tripping over itself. He felt the strongest urge to call his girlfriend, to tell her he was okay and that he missed her, but he didn't. He called the emergency services. He'd found a body, and somewhere out there were loved ones who'd been waiting years or maybe even decades for news of the man whose body was suspended in front of Brett now, like an insect preserved in amber from another age.

One

He was buried in the white and gray depths, so close to the canvas that he could feel and smell the paint, could work its thick contours, but could not see it. Only every now and then would he retreat across the studio to the big old couch, to sit and stare and decide where it needed more work.

The figures would come later. That wasn't usually the case, but for this series he'd experimented with background first, establishing the context before superimposing the subjects. So far it had worked. This was the largest canvas in the series, and already, from the vantage point of the couch, he could imagine the three life-size figures he planned against this dazzlingly pale background. But they could wait.

Foster tipped his head back and looked at the night's deep blue washing out beyond the skylights high above. It was nearly dawn, a fact that filled him with satisfaction, because it meant the painting had come to him, eating up the night without him even realizing.

He cleaned up, then walked out of the studio, switching everything off as he left. He didn't bother turning on the lights as he walked through the open-plan office, either. The subterranean glow from the security light by the main entrance was enough for him to see his way across to the far door that led to his living quarters.

Foster liked the feel of the place at this time of night—or morning—his assistants missing from the office, the entire studio complex empty of the various workers and craftspeople who often came and went throughout the day, the phones silent, the building at peace. Having all of this was a tangible symbol of his success, and yet it was now, in the solitude of these hours, that Foster appreciated it most.

He took the elevator up to the loft apartment. Automatically, he made an effort to keep quiet as he crossed the living space to the kitchen area, even though he knew he no longer needed to be mindful of the noise he made. There was no one to disturb, but it was taking him a while to adjust to that fact.

He drank a glass of water and went into the bedroom, fresh as a hotel room. He'd never liked returning from a night in the studio to a bedroom that was full of sleep, the stale, slightly oppressive air of early morning hanging over it. Yet right now, he kind of missed it, the way he kind of missed even the most annoying things about Nele.

She'd only lived with him for seven months, and even then had kept her own apartment—*because it's a great place and I don't want to lose it if this doesn't work*—yet her absence seemed to have left a bigger hole than the one she'd filled in the first place.

Still, that hadn't been his choice. She'd wanted too much of him, for his work to come second to her, and he hadn't been able to give her that, so she'd left. It was sad, but it was what happened. People left. Sooner or later, people always left. Only the art remained.

Two

It was a little after midday when Foster walked into the office. Maja and Axel were both on calls. Natsuko was working at her computer but turned as he walked in.

"Hey, Foster."

"Hey, Natsuko."

He looked across to the reception area, where a woman was talking quietly into her cellphone. She was young and slim with short dark hair, but the charcoal-gray business suit made her look out of place here. Even so, she waved at Foster when she saw him.

"Who's she?"

"Daniela Herrera, from the American embassy. It's the third time she's been here this morning."

"Really?"

Natsuko nodded. "Really. She was waiting outside when Axel arrived first thing."

"Am I expecting her?"

"Nope."

"She say what it's about?"

"Says it's private." Foster and Natsuko exchanged a glance, acknowledging that Daniela Herrera wasn't from their world, that if she were she'd know there wasn't much that was too private to be handled by his team or his gallerists or PR company. Natsuko handed him a letter then. "This was with the morning mail."

He looked at the printed address on the envelope and pulled the single sheet of paper free. Like the address, the note was printed in Comic Sans, which seemed like a slight in itself. He'd been getting these notes for the last year or more.

You're a fraud and you know it. Your time will come.

He handed it back to Natsuko, who said, "Should I send it across to Sigrid?"

Sigrid was an investigator who'd looked into a couple of matters for him—the theft of an unfinished canvas from the storeroom and the leaking of financial information to a journalist. He'd retained her since to look into any abusive mail he received.

"I'm not so sure this is one for Sigrid. I'm paying her to investigate threats, not criticism."

Was it even criticism? He'd spent most of the last decade feeling like an impostor, as if he'd stolen someone else's success—and not just that of a random someone, but someone in particular.

Natsuko seemed more concerned about the implication of the note's second line and said, "I think this is enough of a threat, especially when you look at it alongside some of the other Comic Sans letters."

"We don't know they're all by the same person," he said. Natsuko raised her eyebrows and Foster smiled in defeat. "Okay, send it across to Sigrid."

He heard the woman end her call and so he strolled across to her. She took a few steps to meet him, her hand outstretched.

"Mr. Treherne, my name's—"

"Miss Herrera, from the embassy. And please, call me Foster."

"Daniela." They shook hands. "Let me say first of all, it's a real honor to meet you, and to be in your studio—I mean, such an amazing building."

She sounded nervous, her voice racing slightly.

"Thanks, it's a former brewery . . . Natsuko said this is your third visit this morning, so I'm guessing it's something pretty important."

"Yes, it is." Her face grew more somber, as if she'd practiced this expression for moments of gravity. "There was an avalanche in Switzerland, day before yesterday, high above the Handeck Glacier, and in the aftermath a body was found, one that's been trapped within the glacier for some time. The details haven't been released yet, but it's your father's body, Mr. Treherne. They've found it."

"I see." He couldn't quite match his tone to the weight Daniela had given her own words.

He'd always known this day might come. His father had been a postgraduate history student at the University of Bologna in Italy, part of a close group of expats who'd enjoyed the mountains; though, crucially, he'd been alone on the day of his disappearance.

That latter fact and its associated air of mystery had offered the only hope throughout Foster's childhood that his dad had disappeared rather than died, transforming him into a fantasy figure. That's whose body had apparently been found, a man who'd only ever truly lived in Foster's imagination.

Daniela looked briefly at the chairs that filled the reception area behind her and said, "Is there somewhere we can discuss the matter?"

Clearly she didn't think this was suitable, even though Natsuko, Maja, and Axel were all far enough away to be pretty much out of earshot. Once again, he wasn't sure what could be so confidential anyway, but even so, he nodded.

9

"Sure. We could go up to the apartment or through to the studio, even though there isn't really anywhere particularly comfortable to sit in there."

"I don't mind not sitting."

Her eyes seemed to light up at the prospect of seeing where he worked, and when he showed her through into the gallery-sized space of the studio she looked around like a kid in a toy store, so rapt that he wondered if Natsuko had checked her ID to make sure she really was from the embassy and not some crazed stalker. But then, he doubted even the craziest stalker would have made up a story about them finding his dad's body.

She pointed at some of the canvases that were nearing completion. "Are these for the exhibition in January?"

"Yes, they are." He looked at them himself, seeing them with fresh eyes. He was happy with them, and was even happy with the newest, the white and gray base that was yet to be developed.

She nodded and turned to look at him, saying, "It's why I volunteered to come and talk with you. I'm such a fan of your work. I was at college when the whole New Painters thing happened, and I was just blown away by it. I knew right then you'd be the breakout star from the show." She stopped, looking embarrassed. "Sorry, hardly an appropriate time to be getting all fangirl with you."

He smiled.

"You can relax. My father disappeared before I was born, and everyone guessed a glacier would spit him out sooner or later. So . . . I guess I'm saying it's fine. Not like you're breaking shocking news."

"Sure, I can understand that. I imagine it's hard to miss someone you've never known."

That was something different, and Foster wasn't sure it was entirely true. He remembered too well the fantasies about his father turning up for him, particularly during his time at Bennington, the boarding school he'd been sent to in New Hampshire. In his dreams there'd always been some amazing explanation—that he'd been working as a spy, that he'd suffered amnesia in a fall—and having no tangible idea of the man his father had been had only allowed the fantasies to be all the richer and the void all the greater.

Even so, he wasn't about to share that with Miss Herrera from the embassy, so he said, "Very true. And thanks for liking my work." He pointed to the couch. "As you can see, that's full of paint, so not wise to sit there, but there are some regular office chairs over by the desk."

"Okay." They walked across and sat down, though her gaze lingered on the paint-spattered couch, as if she might be tempted to sit on it anyway. Once they were sitting she seemed to adopt a more businesslike tone. "So, we always aim to assist US citizens in these kinds of situations, but given your high profile, in this case I've been assigned to assist and facilitate in any way I can. In the first instance, that will mean accompanying you to Bern, should you wish to go. The body was successfully recovered and taken to the Bern Institute for Forensic Medicine."

Foster nodded, grateful for the distraction as Axel came into the studio carrying a tray. A *body* had been taken to a forensic institute—that simple fact was making this seem a lot more real all of a sudden, and the fact that he was the only living person with any direct connection to that body carried a weight he hadn't expected. This was a responsibility, one he'd never even thought to prepare for—his imaginary father had just become a body.

Axel handed a glass to Daniela Herrera as he said, "I know you didn't want coffee, but we're having cinnamon water so I thought you might like some too. I hope you enjoy."

"Er, thank you."

He handed a second glass to Foster.

"Thanks, Axel."

"You're welcome." He turned once more to Daniela. "Can I get you something else?"

"No, this is great, thank you." She watched as Axel padded silently away, then sipped the drink, looking mildly surprised. "Wow, it really is cinnamon water—who knew that was a thing?"

Foster smiled at this glimpse of the person beneath the work suit. He liked her—the way she engaged with things, the way she spoke, the good humor that seemed to underpin her.

"When will they make it public?"

"His identity? Not until they've spoken to you, preferably in person. I understand in these circumstances it's not usual to view the body, though you can discuss that with the director of the institute when you meet with him. It's just a question of arranging a time for you to visit, sooner rather than later if at all possible."

"Sure. I don't think I have anything planned, but you can arrange it with Natsuko. Tomorrow, maybe?"

"That *could* work." She sounded doubtful. "We'd have to check with the institute and take care of the travel arrangements, but—"

"We can take my plane."

"Of course." She laughed. "You're Foster Treherne. Of course you have your own plane."

He laughed too and said, "I know, it's excessive. I also kind of hate it for environmental reasons, but it just makes life a hell of a lot easier."

"I'm sure it does." She took another sip of the drink, then put the glass on the desk. "Well, I better not take up too much of your time right now. It hardly needs saying, but having access to a plane should make things easier to arrange. I'll liaise with Natsuko and hope to see you tomorrow."

She stood and so did Foster, and as he shook her hand again he said, "Thank you for coming."

"Not at all, and I'm sorry for your loss, Foster. It must have been strange all these years, and a strange thing to hear now."

"Thirty-two years."

"Wow. I mean, I knew that, but hearing it spelled out like that—it's two years longer than I've been alive."

"It's seven months longer than *I've* been alive. And . . . he was in the glacier seven years longer than he was alive himself. So yeah, I guess it's pretty strange." She offered a sad smile, but seemed unsure how to respond beyond that, and he could hardly blame her. "Do you mind showing yourself out? You know where to find Natsuko."

"Of course. And I'll be in touch."

He stood motionless as he listened to her footsteps retreat across the gallery floor, then as she walked through the double doors. He wasn't sure what he was meant to feel right now. He hadn't known the man, had spent most of his life purposefully avoiding finding out too much about either of the parents who'd abandoned him in one way or another.

They had found his father, dead after all. Foster turned, seeing the new canvas and noting that it looked like a vast glacial landscape. Daniela Herrera might have interpreted it in exactly that way, as a lost boy searching through the icy wastes for the father he'd never known.

And maybe she'd believed she was bringing him some kind of closure here today, bringing news that would finally fill part of the void. But the strange hope he'd carried through his childhood had long since eroded, leaving behind only a stone worn smooth. The discovery of a body could hardly change that—and worse, it would most likely just lead to a renewal of the ghoulish curiosity that had plagued him his whole career.

ART FRONTIERS APRIL/MAY, 2019

Words by Miriam Donald

The Little Boy Lost of American Art

Within ten years of bursting onto the scene with The New Painters, Foster Treherne has firmly established himself in the top tier of American artists on the world stage, staking a credible claim to being the leading figurative painter of his generation. It's not difficult to see why. Beyond the rich color fields and textural complexity, his canvases are imbued with a profound sense of loneliness and desolation that speaks directly to the human condition in the 21st century. It may be born out of the artist's uniquely tragic background, but it gives voice to the existential reality we all face. We are lost, Treherne appears to be telling us, and we are all alone.

Three

It was a twenty-minute ride into Bern from the airport. The city was bathed in sunshine but even the lower slopes of the surrounding hills and mountains were still snow-covered from the recent fall.

Daniela said, "So the man we're going to see is Professor Martin Dorn. He's the director of the institute."

Foster nodded, correcting her in his own mind—the man he was going to see was Charles Treherne.

"Have you been to Bern before?"

Foster said, "Couple times. I had an exhibition at the Kunstmuseum, and then they found out I'm a fan of Adolf Wölfli, so they invited me back for a retrospective of his work."

"Were you tempted, when you were here, to go visit the glacier?"

The question reminded him of Polly, his girlfriend through art school in London. She was the only other person who'd ever asked him if he'd thought about visiting the glacier, searching for the body, and she hadn't understood his refusal even to discuss it. His fantasies had never been about being the one who found the body; they'd always been about there being no body at all.

"Honestly, it never even occurred to me that it was close by. I know it's in the Bernese Alps, but is it near the city?"

"No, I don't think it's very close, maybe two hours. I just wondered."

He understood her curiosity, and he could also see why she might fail to understand his lack of it.

"I guess if I'd known him at all it might have been different. And it wasn't like I would've known where to look. Apparently he didn't tell anyone where he was walking that day, and even if he had, I think the glacier is pretty big."

"I believe so." She turned back to the view through the window. He liked the center of Bern but, even in the sunshine, the suburb they were driving through was nondescript, and he detected a note of disappointment as she said, "I've never been to Switzerland at all before."

"I like it. Even thought about setting up a studio here for a while. I'm in Zurich and Basel regularly."

She nodded and smiled politely, but he was struggling to converse with her. The day before, when she'd been breaking bad news to him—or good news, depending on the viewpoint—she'd been nervous to begin with, then natural and easygoing. Today, apart from the question about him visiting the glacier, she'd been talking like someone using a script, as if she'd been reprimanded for being too familiar with a VIP.

He was tempted to remind her that he was no such thing, but before he could say anything else she said, "There's already been some speculation in the local media about the identity of the body, some of it mentioning your father, as you'd imagine. There's been nothing back home yet."

The word "home" jarred in Foster's thoughts. Where was home? What was home? A studio in Berlin, another in New York, a house in London he visited no more than once a year, another in Miami that he'd been to only once. Those were his houses, but where was his home?

Daniela continued, saying, "But as I mentioned yesterday, once they've spoken to you, the identity will be released. You can expect considerable media interest at that point."

"My gallerists will be thrilled." The joke fell flat, and in truth, it wasn't much of a joke—both Claudia and Werner would trade on the news story in their own way. He turned to look at her. "Where's your home, Daniela, if you don't mind me asking?"

"Um . . ." As if backing up his earlier theory, she looked like someone aware she was about to venture off-script. "It's not that exciting. I was raised in Denver. My dad was born in Guadalajara but moved to California when he was two, moved to Colorado after college to work at Lockheed Martin, met my mom."

"She's from Denver?"

"Boulder. Her parents were both professors at the university." Daniela smiled. "We still go to their house for Thanksgiving every year, me and my brothers. Well, I missed last year, couldn't get home, but you know . . ."

He nodded, though he didn't know, not about any of it. His grandparents should have been the windows into where he'd come from and who he was, but neither set had apparently cared to take ownership of that legacy. And Thanksgiving had always been the one holiday that made him feel about as un-American as it was possible to feel.

"You sound close, I like that. My mother was English."

"Yeah. Yeah, I knew that."

Of course she knew that. She knew that his mother was English, that she'd met his dad studying at Bologna, where they'd been part of the same group of friends, that she'd killed herself when he was a year old, that her name had been Lucy Foster, and that she'd chosen to hand down the curse of both his parental lines by calling him Foster Treherne.

Daniela knew all of it because it was public knowledge, and it sounded romantic enough that she felt her own background wasn't interesting by comparison. And she could have no idea how much he envied those Thanksgiving obligations, and brothers or sisters, and a life that could easily be dismissed as too regular to be of interest.

The car pulled up at the institute, a large and functional modern building in an otherwise leafy residential neighborhood. They made their way to the front desk, where they were asked for ID and told to take a seat.

The plush reception area was like that of a multinational company rather than an academic institution. Neither of them sat down, and neither of them spoke.

A few minutes later, a man came out to them, wearing a dark suit and frameless glasses, his short fair hair neatly styled. His appearance reinforced the impression that they were here to discuss an investment opportunity rather than a thirty-two-year-old corpse, but it seemed this was their man.

"Mr. Treherne, Miss Herrera, I'm Professor Martin Dorn, director of the institute."

As they shook hands, Foster said, "Good to meet you, Professor."

Daniela added, "And thanks for seeing us at such short notice."

"Not at all." He smiled, full of warmth. "In fact, this case was one of the easy ones. With some historic discoveries the identity is not clear, or the victims are so old that the relatives are no longer alive. But please, come through to my office."

They followed him down a long featureless corridor, the doors all closed, and then into a spacious modern office. An inner door was open into another room, and he leaned through and gave an instruction to his secretary, then closed the door.

"Please, sit down." As Foster sat, he noticed there was a box of Kleenex on the leather-topped desk, presumably for the relatives of less historic cases. "And before we begin, I hope you don't mind . . ." Dorn opened a drawer and took out a large book. "Do you mind, a signature?"

It was the official catalogue for the exhibition at the Kunstmuseum.

"Not at all. Did you go?"

"We did, and enjoyed it very much, but I must confess, it's my wife who is the big fan of art."

"Would you like me to sign it to her?"

"That's too kind. Angelika, with a 'k.'"

Professor Dorn watched, smiling the whole time, as Foster wrote and signed a dedication to his wife. He took back the catalogue and studied the inscription before putting it back in the drawer.

"She'll be so happy." He sat down now, then opened another drawer in his desk and took out a heavy brown envelope. He placed it on the desk in front of him, but instead of opening it, he looked across at Foster. "So, I understand your father disappeared in October, thirty-two years ago."

"That's correct. Seven months before I was born."

"Of course. It's near the end of the popular summer hiking season, but that October there had been unexpected heavy snowfall, and it was snowing even on the day he set out. His companion who was visiting the area with him didn't walk that day, and told the authorities that your father didn't indicate the route he planned to take. Naturally, this oversight made the search much more difficult, although there's no guarantee he would have been found in these conditions anyway."

Foster knew that his father had been in the area with a friend but that he'd been walking alone that day. He couldn't recall the friend's name, if he'd ever known it, but he knew he'd been one of the close group that had formed that year in Bologna. The only important facts for Foster were that his father had been alone and that he'd disappeared.

"I know they mounted an extensive search for him."

Professor Dorn nodded solemnly, and said, "Yes. I was still a child at the time, but I clearly remember this case." He paused, as if to let that point sink in, that only one of the people in this room had been alive when Charles Treherne died on the Handeck Glacier, and even he had been a child. "What we now know is that he fell and was buried in the glacier. The site is above the accumulation zone, which ensured the——"

Daniela cut in. "Excuse me, Professor, the 'accumulation zone'?"

"My apologies. The lower part of a glacier is the ablation zone, where the ice mass is gradually lost due to summer melting and other natural factors. The higher part is the accumulation zone, where snowfall generally exceeds what is lost through those same processes. This is important because the location ensured the preservation of the body in the condition it was found after the avalanche a few days ago."

"How did you know it was my father?"

Dorn patted the envelope, then slid it across the desk to Foster.

"These were inside the backpack—his passport and a journal or diary. Both were also wrapped inside a plastic bag, which, as you'll see, preserved them perfectly."

Foster took the envelope and slid the contents out onto the desk. An American passport, and a journal. He took the notebook and flicked through the pages, looking at the dense script without reading any of it, feeling he didn't even want to read it, to know his father's thoughts—even though he'd never known the man, it felt like an intrusion. He picked up the passport then, but put it down again without opening it.

"I'd like to see the body."

"I thought you might say this. I would advise against it. Although your father's body was very well preserved by the ice, it was damaged by the fall and by the movement of the glacier, and even at those temperatures, after thirty-two years . . . What I mean to say is, viewing the body can destroy the memory people have of their loved one. A body recovered from a glacier, it's not the best memory to keep."

"I have no memories, Professor Dorn, none at all. For me, anything is better than nothing."

"I understand, and I prepared for this." Dorn stood. "As long as you acknowledge my reservations."

"I do."

Foster stood too, but Daniela said, "I'll sit this one out, if you don't mind."

He looked at her and smiled. He'd have been more suspicious if she'd wanted to come. He wasn't entirely sure why he wanted to see the body himself, except perhaps to be confident that this was the end, the conclusion of a mystery that had quietly dominated most of his life.

Four

Foster had expected to be taken to a morgue, the body pulled out from a wall of metal drawers, but Dorn actually took him to a glass-walled laboratory. He'd also expected it to smell strongly of formaldehyde, but there was only a faintly detectable scent of disinfectant.

In the middle of the room was what looked like an operating table, with a sheet draped over what was clearly a body. On the far side of the room was a long metal shelf containing various items of clothing and other, indistinguishable, objects.

Professor Dorn walked across to that far side, ignoring the body even as he moved around it, and said, "Perhaps you would like to see these things first. Many had to be cut to avoid damage to the body in their removal, but you can see here your father's backpack, together with its other contents—water bottle, candy bar, a pen, spare socks—and his hiking boots, his jacket."

Foster stared at the bright red of the jacket, so vibrant it almost looked new, as if his father might rise up off the table and ask for it back. There was a plaid shirt next to it, neatly folded. Foster could see it was missing three buttons in a row, the threads of cotton clearly visible where the buttons had been, as if they'd been torn free only minutes before.

Dorn waited patiently as Foster moved along the shelf, then cleared his throat.

"I ask one more time, Mr. Treherne, you still wish to view the body?"

Foster nodded and turned to the figure behind him on the table.

Dorn walked around the table so that he was facing Foster, and carefully pulled the sheet down from the head, resting it across the top of the torso so it resembled a bedsheet covering a hospital patient.

Foster had to fight an urge to step back, because he had asked to see this, and it wasn't so much that it horrified him, more that it was not as he'd expected. At first it looked like the shrunken head of an old man, tufts of his father's fair hair visible on the tightly stretched scalp, the ears apparently missing. But the face itself—eyes and mouth closed—looked disturbingly youthful, the skin pale and smooth, a young man at rest.

"I . . ." He'd seen pictures of his father, a good-looking guy—a breezy confident swagger about him, usually with a smile. And it took Foster a moment, but he could see that person here in these ice-tautened features that were turned slightly toward him. He did not look as he had looked in life, but he looked close enough for it to seem impossible that more than three decades had elapsed.

Foster glanced at the sheet where it covered the rest of the body, at the odd peaks and troughs and contours.

As if reading his mind, Professor Dorn said, "I really would strongly advise not to view any more of it."

Foster nodded, but said, "His body was broken like that by the fall?"

"We can say with some certainty that a leg and some of the ribs were broken in the fall. Where the body is badly misshapen, it's more from the movement of the glacier. It's fortunate that the head was positioned in such a way that it was left relatively unscathed."

"Do you know . . . I mean, did he freeze to death or die from the impact or . . ."

Professor Dorn pointed to the back of the skull, and Foster noticed now that it was darkened and malformed.

"With this kind of incident, many injuries are caused in a short space of time, and it's not always easy to ascertain the order or the importance of each individual injury. However, there was a blunt force trauma to the back of the head, causing significant damage to the skull and the soft tissue beneath, and the blood patterns on the surrounding tissue and on the backpack and the collar of his jacket all suggest it was either the direct cause of death or a major contributing factor."

"So you think he fell, hit his head on a rock, and that was it?"

"It's impossible to say for sure, but that would seem a likely scenario."

Foster moved around to the same side of the table as Dorn, and looked more closely at the darkened flesh of the wound on the back of his father's head.

"Looks like someone hit him with something."

He felt stupid even as he said it, because this was the first body he'd ever seen, a body that had fallen down a mountain and then been mashed up by a glacier.

But Dorn said, "Yes, I can see that, and naturally, we consider the possibility of a crime when we compile our report into the cause of death, but it's rare in these cases, and the injury you see here—as well as the underlying damage—is entirely consistent with falling against a sharp outcrop of rock."

Foster nodded acceptance, and he hadn't seriously believed his father had been struck with an ice axe or some other weapon—he'd just been trying to make conversation in a situation that didn't allow for it.

There was no reason at all for Foster to imagine his father had been the victim of a crime, but now that the subject had arisen, he felt obliged to say, "So it was definitely an accident."

Dorn smiled sympathetically. "After thirty-two years, very little is definite. As far as we know, nobody else was on the mountain that day, which makes our job easier. There were some minor indications that your father had been involved in some sort of altercation—let's call it a scuffle—some time before the fall, but it could have been the night before, or earlier that morning. Again, if someone had been on the mountain, they might have had some questions to answer, but no more than that."

Foster looked down at the face, at the landscape of the body. "What kind of indications?"

"Minor. Three buttons were missing from his shirt, suggesting it had been torn open." Dorn demonstrated by dragging his hand across his own chest. "The sweatshirt beneath wasn't *noticeably* damaged but there are two slight abrasions on the chest, consistent with fingernails being dragged rapidly across the area. Unfortunately, his jacket was unzipped when we found him."

"Why, what does that indicate?"

"Directly, it indicates that it was warm—after all, it was October, not January—and that he'd been climbing hard. What I meant was that if his jacket had been zipped, we might have assumed the shirt was torn before he set out, and that's still the most likely scenario—"

"Because no one else was on the mountain."

"Exactly. But even then . . ." Dorn paused, as if wanting to be sure of choosing the right words. "You know, even if someone had been with him, minor fights or squabbles among hiking and climbing companions are relatively common, and as I said, it might have raised questions but wouldn't, of itself, suggest foul play. As it is, his travel companion didn't hike with him that day, citing illness, so maybe they fought beforehand and *that's* why they didn't walk together. It's one possibility."

"So they had a fight, a scuffle, and my dad went out alone."

"Exactly," said Dorn, his regretful expression managing to capture all the subsequent possibilities—that he had been alone, with no one to cover his back or question the wisdom of proceeding in worsening weather, that he had still been angry maybe, not thinking straight. "I'm sure there's nothing more to it than that. A little mystery that perhaps can never be solved, but sad, too."

"Yes."

Foster looked one more time at his father, apparently sleeping, old and young simultaneously, that little mystery of three missing buttons locked away forever in those passive features, and said, "You can cover him back up now, thank you."

Dorn rearranged the sheet and said, "I hope you didn't find this too upsetting."

"No, I'm glad I saw him." For the first and last time, thought Foster. He glanced back at the white mountain-scape of the body beneath that sheet, and one final question came to him. "I guess the friend he was traveling with would have been interviewed at the time?"

"Of course, and also the owner of the *pension* where they stayed. I've read the reports and there's nothing untoward within them. The owner of the *pension* confirmed that your father's friend didn't go out that day."

Foster nodded, but he thought of those threads standing proud from the shirt, almost as if the buttons had been pulled loose in just the last few minutes, and in his own mind he could only imagine this scuffle happening in the place where his father had fallen to his death. Did that mean anything, and hadn't his imagination betrayed him too many times when it came to his father?

"I guess I just want to be sure it really was an accident."

Dorn looked back at the body too, and sighed. "I think an accident most likely, don't you? The alternative we'd have to consider is that your father encountered a stranger during a snowstorm, a stranger who proceeded to get into a fight with him and throw him to his death."

"Or that his friend was lying." Even as he said it, he cursed himself—Charles Treherne hadn't been pushed to his death, just as he hadn't been a spy or suffering from amnesia all these years.

As if backing up that inner voice, Dorn said patiently, "If his friend lied, so did the owner of the *pension*. I think that's not so plausible. And for you, better to believe the most likely sequence, that he strayed from the path in heavy snow, fell, hit the back of his head on a sharp edge of rock, and continued on into a final impact with the glacier. No death on the mountain is a good death, Mr. Treherne, and he was too young, but it would have been quick, and you must also remember that people who die on mountains generally die in a place they love."

Dorn was right. Of course he was right, and Foster's desperate grasping after deeper truths was probably just a sign that this had affected him more profoundly than he'd imagined possible.

Foster said, "I like to think that. I didn't know him, but it's still good to think he was somewhere he wanted to be when it happened."

"I'm glad you can feel that way." Dorn gestured toward the door in the glass wall. "Please."

They left, but Foster looked back one last time once they were in the corridor. He wasn't sure why, except maybe as a final farewell. In one way or another, it was as if they had both been trapped in that glacier these last three decades, and maybe in one way or another, they would both also now be free of it.

Five

Daniela stood as they walked back into the office. She looked expectant, with a level of concern that Foster found touching, given how little they knew each other.

"It wasn't as bad as you'd imagine."

Dorn added, "No, the circumstances were fortunate in many respects. It's unusual for the preservation to be of such a high level."

"I'm glad." Daniela smiled apologetically, saying, "I still didn't want to see it. I hope you understand."

"Of course." They sat down and Foster said to Dorn, "So what happens now?"

"We can finish our reports; the identity of the deceased will be made public. Miss Herrera has already dealt with many of the details, so quite soon we'll be able to release the body."

"Release?"

As if he'd imagined it to be obvious, Dorn said, "For the funeral."

"Oh, sure."

Foster hadn't thought about that, the fact that even a thirty-two-year-old corpse needed some form of ceremonial interment.

"Well, thanks for your time, Professor Dorn."

"I've been happy to help. I'll show you out, but don't forget those." He pointed to the notebook and passport, and Foster picked them up and slipped them back inside the envelope.

Once they were outside, he said to Daniela, "We have a couple of hours to spare, if you'd like to see the city center, maybe get some lunch. The old town's quite something."

"Sure, I'd like that."

He had the car drop them near the Zytglogge tower, and they found a restaurant in one of the covered arcades. It was only when they were sitting down that he finally took the passport out and looked at the picture inside.

His dad had been fairer than him, and the picture had been taken three years before his death, but it was still a shock to see the boyish face staring out at him, a reminder that Charles Treherne had died a young man, six years younger than Foster was now. It was hard, too, to reconcile the picture in the passport with the otherworldly face he'd seen at the institute.

Daniela interrupted his thoughts before they had the chance to turn maudlin, saying, "I'm guessing from your response back at the institute that you haven't given much thought to the funeral?"

He put the passport away again and looked up at her as he said, "It was that obvious, huh?"

"Obvious, but also completely understandable." A waiter approached their table. They hadn't even looked at their menus yet, so with a smile, Daniela waved him away and the waiter retreated, looking a little smitten by her. "Have you any idea about where he might have wanted to be buried?"

"I doubt the average twenty-five-year-old gives it much thought."

"No. Maybe the town where he was raised or . . . I get that you didn't know him, but you must have heard something about him from—"

"My mother?" It had come out more flippant than he'd intended. Daniela looked embarrassed and lowered her head slightly, and Foster said, "Sorry, force of habit. It's just weird going through life with people knowing so much about my personal history."

"I can understand that, too. And I was really thinking of other family members. I mean, you were raised by somebody, right?"

He nodded. That was one way of putting it.

"My paternal grandparents didn't even recognize me as their own until I was ten. Apparently I always looked a lot like him, but some DNA testing was done for their peace of mind, not that it made much difference to our relationship. My maternal grandparents left me almost exclusively in the care of an American nanny. They let her go once I was old enough to be sent to Bennington— that's the boarding school in New Hampshire that my dad went to. They didn't want me to lose touch with my American heritage."

"What about your English heritage?"

He shrugged. "In their defense, their only daughter had a breakdown after giving birth to me and killed herself a year later. That must have been tough for them."

"But you were a *child*. It must have been tougher for you." She looked outraged on his behalf.

"Maybe. They're all dead now anyway. Abigail still comes to most of my US openings."

"Abigail?"

"The nanny."

He smiled at a memory, of when he'd first gone to kindergarten in the village in Berkshire where his grandparents had lived, and how, hearing the other kids talking to their mothers, he'd started calling Abigail "Mummy." Abigail had found it funny, even as she'd corrected him, but one day his grandmother had overheard and said quite coldly, "You have no mummy—she's gone to heaven." His smile fell away again at that part of the memory.

Daniela said, "I'm honestly at a loss, and naturally I'm in no position to suggest what your father might have wanted, but if you need help with any of the formalities, I'll do all I can to help."

"I appreciate that, and I appreciate you coming here with me today." He picked up his menu. "But let's forget about it all for now. Let's eat."

She picked up her menu too, and in truth, it was easy for Foster to put thoughts of a funeral out of his mind, because he didn't have many thoughts on the subject anyway. After all, how was he meant to organize a funeral for someone he hadn't known, someone with whom he really had no connection at all?

If his father's body had been found at the time he died, Foster's grandparents would have organized the funeral. Maybe Lucy—the girlfriend carrying their unborn grandchild—would have been involved, maybe the others in his close group of friends at Bologna.

Foster thought of those friends now. With the exception of Lucy, they were probably all still alive, in their late fifties. But then, even if Foster had any way of identifying or contacting them, he could hardly get in touch to ask what kind of funeral his dad would have wanted.

He also wondered if they'd really been all that close anyway, and with that, a nagging thought returned, of those three missing buttons and the scratches beneath. Foster had never been one for fighting, but maybe Charles had. Or it might not have been a real fight at all, just drunken horseplay that had gotten out of hand.

The only definitive fact was that someone had torn his father's shirt at some point in the hours before his death. That person was still out there somewhere, the *only* person who knew how significant an act it had been.

And for the first time, Foster found himself curious about his dad's life—not the fantasy figure who'd never come back, but the young man he'd actually been; curious about the days and weeks beforehand, curious about his time in Bologna, a period that had culminated in some kind of altercation and a fateful decision to hike that isolated mountain trail.

Six

What a night it was last night. Seriously! This is kind of what I'd hoped for and never found at Yale. It's not just that they're great people, it's that they GET IT. G and H both very cool. And smart— they're all smart. I told them what I'd discovered about the cemetery in Livorno and they were all completely into it—we're going early next week. Oh, and then there's L!! She's English and . . . well, maybe I should just leave it at that.

Foster had flown back, had the car drop Daniela at her apartment in Kreuzberg, then returned home early evening. Yet the same emptiness that he usually savored had jarred somehow, because he wanted someone to ask him how his trip had been, how it felt to view the body of his long-dead father.

He'd gone into the studio for a few hours, working on every canvas except for the one he now struggled to think of as anything but a glacier, then went to bed and slept fitfully until midmorning. Since waking, he'd been looking through his father's journal, deciphering the neat but densely packed handwriting.

Foster's instant response, and one that lingered, was an envy for this world of close college bonds, of all-consuming friendships, of spirited adventures. The irony was that Foster and his own select group of friends at Goldsmiths had all been too obsessed with business and making it big to waste time on what they saw as childish pursuits.

Passion, as they'd seen it, was just one more thing that could be measured and monetized. And that probably explained why Foster now had half a million followers on Instagram but an empty apartment, above an almost-empty studio complex.

This group of expat postgraduates at Bologna had been swept up in each other. There was lots of talk of the mountains in his dad's journal, as Foster would have expected, but also of libraries and cemeteries and ancient churches, of "feasts" and "banquets" rather than dinners, of "gatherings" rather than parties.

In places, it read evocatively enough that Foster could readily picture it:

> *Explored the San Lorenzo Catacombs late last night. Eerie but beautiful, like being lost in another world, another age. We used candles to light one of the small former chapels, hewn right out of the rock, and sat down there, lounging around on the bare floor, and drank a few bottles of the most amazing Sassicaia, talking about life. So happy right now.*

The journal also lapsed occasionally into pretentious juvenilia—*we are drinking deep of history, engaged in a noble endeavor. Et in Arcadia ego*—even less excusable given that they'd been in their mid-twenties by the time his father was writing it. And if he were still alive, maybe the older Charles Treherne would have found the language embarrassing. Yet Foster envied it all the same, envied that feeling of being swept up in a close-knit society of friends.

Once again, he wondered where they all were now, and how they'd respond to the news that the body had been found. Would it bring back happy memories or sad, or maybe, for one of them at least, a fear that the body might bring to light something they'd long thought hidden?

Unfortunately for Foster, his father referred to everyone in his journal by initials alone. With the exception of L—Lucy Foster, his mother—he had nothing to guide him to their identities.

Foster skipped to the last entry. None was dated, so it was impossible to know how long a period of time this notebook covered, or how great the gaps were between various entries. It was reasonably safe to assume that the final page had been written before the trip on which he'd died. But it also went some way to explaining why Charles had been alone that day, and maybe even hinted at the more fractious atmosphere that both Foster and Professor Dorn had imagined in the buildup to the disappearance.

> *Increasingly convinced that P isn't good for any of us.*
> *Also getting a little concerned about how controlling*
> *G has become, how jealous, borderline creepy. As for*
> *this trip, I'm still looking forward to it, but you know,*
> *we were all meant to be going, and now look. Just two*
> *of us! Okay, I understand L wanting to go back to*
> *England. But as for the others . . . it's done, I guess.*
> *Nothing lasts forever.*

There were another twenty or thirty pages left in the book, but they were all pristine, still awaiting the dissection of the trip to Handeck and the fallout from the friends drifting apart. From Foster's vantage point, even that cooling-off had a romantic sepia tint about it.

Of course, Lucy had gone back to England because she was pregnant, probably wanting to be under the care of her own family doctor, the same practice Foster had been taken to with various childhood ailments. He could easily imagine how his grandparents would have reacted to their twenty-three-year-old daughter returning home pregnant from Italy—they'd have taken it in their stride, showing no emotion whatsoever, probably feeling none either.

He wondered who P and G were. G had gone from being "very cool" early on to being "controlling" and "jealous" and "borderline creepy" by the end. P hadn't been mentioned at all to begin with. He or she first appeared after the trip to Livorno—a trip which was frustratingly mentioned only in passing—and had quickly seemed to become the galvanizing member of the group. Yet by the end, Foster's dad had become convinced that P was a bad influence in some way.

What if P or G had also been the person who'd traveled with Charles to Switzerland but had failed to hike that day? If that were the case, he was possibly the only one of the group Foster needed to identify, because if he'd lied about not hiking on the day of the disappearance, or if he'd lied about fighting with Charles, then maybe this turned into a different story.

Foster closed the notebook, suddenly doubting himself. This had happened in the 1980s, not the 1880s. He was pretty sure the authorities must have considered the possibility his father hadn't really been alone, and they must have discounted it. But then, the authorities had been investigating the disappearance of a hiker in a snowstorm, not the death of a young man who might have fought with someone in the hours before his death.

Nor did they have access to a notebook that voiced concerns about some of his friends—about G, who was becoming borderline creepy, about P who was no longer good for any of them. Would it have changed things if they had?

The phone rang next to the bed, the sound so alarming in the quiet of the loft that he jumped, and his heart was still cantering as he answered.

It was Natsuko.

"Sorry to disturb you, Foster, but Daniela Herrera is here to see you."

He looked at the clock. It was almost midday.

"I'll be down shortly."

Foster headed into the shower, but as he let the water pour over him, he kept thinking of his father's alien face, simultaneously wizened and eternally youthful. *Nothing lasts forever*, he'd written in his prophetic final words, but his life had not been meant to end there on that day.

Dorn had stressed that a crime seemed unlikely, and Foster was mistrustful of his own instincts, but the urge to look into this was still strong. He wanted to know who had fought with his father, and when, and whether that person had a case to answer. That was all, and he imagined any normal son would feel exactly the same.

Seven

Natsuko, Maja, and Axel were sitting in the reception area, looking through blowups of publicity photographs as they ate their lunch.

"Hey Foster," they called out, more or less as one.

"Good morning, all." He glanced at the desks as he walked past, noticing the flashing lights on the phones.

The glance was spotted, and Natsuko said, "We've stopped answering the phones this morning."

He smiled. "Hey, I saw them flashing, that's all. How you run things is up to you."

Maja said, "Not really. It's your life, after all."

"I guess so. What's going on with the phones, anyway?"

Natsuko said, "The news broke about your father, so there are a lot of people wanting comments, interviews. I guessed you wouldn't want any of it."

"Good. I might need to reschedule some things too."

"Already done. You had an interview with *Gagosian* planned for tomorrow—they send their condolences and said they'll push you back to the next issue. Werner was coming Monday to look at the new paintings—I've put him back a week or two, but we're still eight months out, so he's cool with that."

"Great." Foster looked around. "Where's Daniela?"

Axel said, "In the studio. I thought as you met her in there last time. I gave her coffee. She didn't want anything to eat. How about you?"

"I'm okay, thanks. Maybe some coffee but—"

"There's an extra cup already in there."

Foster nodded and walked through to the studio. Axel had clearly been into the storeroom and grabbed some furniture, because there were a couple of small armchairs either side of a coffee table, which was laden with a pot of coffee, two cups, and a plate of cookies. Daniela was sitting facing the latest canvas, but stood when she heard him come in.

He was ambushed by how happy he was to see her. It wasn't just that she was attractive, but more some indefinable quality that made him feel more at ease when she was there. He reminded himself that she was here to do a job and that her own admiration of Foster Treherne probably began and ended with his art.

"Good morning, Daniela." He pointed at the furniture. "I like what you've done with the place."

"Axel was insistent I should be comfortable."

"He's used to moving stuff around."

They sat down and she poured coffee into the two cups as she said, "I was looking at that big canvas, trying to figure out what it will be. And then I wondered, do you know in advance, or do you just feel your way?"

"A little of both. I kind of know what I want to do with it, but that could change as I work." He looked across at it himself, but turned back immediately. "I'm kind of disturbed by how much it resembles a glacial landscape at the moment."

"I was wondering about that too."

"Coincidence. I can say with hand on heart that until you came to the studio the other day, I hadn't given any thought to my father's disappearance for . . . well, as long as I can remember."

She nodded, sipped at her coffee, then said, "This is really a courtesy call to see if there's anything you need right now, but I did some checking. Your dad grew up in Hopton, Connecticut. His family has lived there for generations."

"Yeah, I knew that."

Despite the early refusal to acknowledge Foster as one of their own, and despite the fact they'd never once invited him to stay for Thanksgiving or Christmas or any of the other holidays while he'd been at Bennington Academy, he'd actually inherited the family home seven years ago—the last of the Trehernes. He'd sold it shortly afterwards without ever once setting foot in it.

"So I was thinking, maybe he could be buried there."

"Makes sense, I guess. His parents are buried there."

"Your grandparents."

"Yeah." He could see she was reading something into Foster's apparent refusal to acknowledge his relationship to his own grandparents, so he said, "They came to visit me when I was at Bennington, four times in total, over seven years. My grandfather would shake my hand at both the beginning and end of each visit; my grandmother patted me on the shoulder. So, I think you could call it an understatement to say we weren't close."

"Wow." She looked visibly taken aback. "No disrespect, but it doesn't sound like you had much luck with either set of grandparents."

"You could say that." He smiled. "I like to think it's because I represented something traumatic for them. But who knows, maybe that was the world my parents grew up in, too." He thought about it, then said, "I told you the other day I didn't miss my father because I didn't know any better—well, that wasn't true. I didn't know what it was to have parents, but I knew what it looked like, how it was for all the other kids. I knew enough of what I was missing. But I didn't have anything to compare my grandparents with, and they were never mean to me, they were just . . ."

"Distant?"

"I was gonna say hands-off, but yeah, 'distant' will do."

The studio door opened and Natsuko came in carrying a tablet.

She waited until she'd reached them before saying, "Sorry to disturb, but today's *New York Times* is the first out with the story. Thought you'd want to see it."

"Thanks." He took the tablet from her and looked at the headline and the opening words.

> ICE BODY IS LEADING ARTIST'S LONG-LOST FATHER—*A grisly find in the Swiss Alps has finally solved the mystery disappearance of Charles Treherne, an American postgraduate student at the University of Bologna in Italy, who failed to return from a mountain hike thirty-two years ago. Treherne was the father of the leading American figurative painter Foster Treherne, whose tragic early life . . .*

Foster felt himself almost physically recoil from the words. He didn't want to read yet again of his "tragic early life" or the "cruel blow fate had handed him" or the "sadness and dislocation manifest in all his work."

It was a relief to hear Natsuko say, "I *love* your necklace, Daniela!"

Foster looked up. He'd noticed it in passing as he'd joined her, but looked properly now. It was made up of small rectangular enamels in different colors, suggestive of something Aztec.

"Thank you." She raised her hand and touched the necklace where it lay on the smooth skin beneath her throat, as if she'd forgotten what she was wearing and had to touch it to remind herself.

"There isn't much room for self-expression in my office wardrobe, so I jump at any chance to lift things when I can."

"So pretty." Natsuko turned back to Foster, pointing at the tablet. "There's a picture, too."

He scrolled down to the picture, a group photo from his dad's student days that was immediately, if hazily, familiar. Nine years ago, when his paternal grandfather had died, his grandmother had sent Foster some boxes of his dad's stuff, on the grounds she "wouldn't be around forever," a prophecy she'd fulfilled within two years.

At the time, Foster had leafed idly through the contents of the boxes—from Bennington, Yale, Bologna—before storing them. He remembered a copy of this picture had been among the various papers and photographs and mementoes in the Bologna box. As a twenty-two-year-old, it hadn't interested him, had even made him angry in some undefined way. Now, it fascinated him, not so much because of his parents, though they were both there, standing next to each other, but because of the glimpse it gave into a different world.

This was that close-knit group of friends who'd apparently done everything together for a while, from hiking in the mountains to exploring ancient libraries and monuments. Each of these people probably had a corresponding initial in his dad's journal. And somewhere, even in that captured moment, there were invisible fault lines too.

The six people in the photograph all looked fresh-faced, standing on the interior steps of what appeared to be a chapel or some other ancient building. They had the relaxed air about them of close friends, and were all dressed more like the youth of the 1920s than the 1980s—his father and one of the other men were wearing jackets and ties, not as if they'd dressed up for a special dinner, but as if this were their normal way of dressing.

Underneath the picture, the caption gave his father's name, together with his position in the picture—*far left*—but the only other person named was not Foster's mother, but Chris Hamblyn—*back right*—the other man who was wearing a tie. Why had they named him?

Foster skimmed through the article until he spotted the name again, and now he understood. Chris Hamblyn was a journalist, at the Rome bureau of the *New York Times*. There was a quote from him, saying, "Charlie was such a great guy, and a lot of fun to be around. This news brings back a lot of the sadness I felt at the time of his disappearance, but so many happy memories, too, and hopefully some closure at last for his family."

Foster nodded. People never spoke ill of the dead, but those words sounded genuine enough, that his dad had been a great guy and a lot of fun to be around, the kind of person whose disappearance might leave his friends bereft. Foster liked to think so, anyway.

He thought back to his dad's journal. There had been no "C" that he remembered, but H had been mentioned a few times, so maybe that's who this was, Chris Hamblyn.

Foster looked up at Daniela, then at Natsuko, and pointed at the screen, even though he'd scrolled past the picture now.

"This guy, Chris Hamblyn, he's in Rome, working for the *New York Times*. I'd like to meet him if I could."

Natsuko looked surprised, and said, "You want to give an interview?"

"No. God, no. He speaks really highly of my father, so maybe he'll wanna come to the funeral. And he might know where the other people in this picture are—maybe they'd come too."

He looked down again and scrolled back to the photograph. As well as his parents and Chris Hamblyn, there were two women, and a guy who looked like he might be Italian, wearing a white shirt and a cravat. Could that third man be G or P—and even if he weren't, would Chris Hamblyn be able to tell Foster whose initials those had been?

Foster realized, as he thought about it, that he was becoming increasingly drawn to the idea that his father hadn't died entirely by accident, even though Professor Dorn had been at pains to say it couldn't be proven either way. He felt a deeply ingrained obligation to find out for sure, an obligation to the man smiling languidly out from that photograph, a man who had the look about him of someone Foster might have liked.

Natsuko said, "I should be able to get his contact details easily enough."

"Okay, and forward the picture to Sigrid. It's a long shot, but ask her if she can help identify the others in the photograph, just in case Chris Hamblyn can't help us."

He handed the tablet back to Natsuko and she said, "I'll get right on it."

She left, but then Daniela said, "Well, I don't want to take up any more of your time. I should be able to liaise with your office on any remaining matters, but if you do need anything, don't hesitate to get in touch." She took a card out and gave it to him. "I left one with Natsuko, too, but call me if you need anything."

"Thanks. And thanks for stopping by."

She lingered for a moment, as if about to say something else, a pause that seemed full of some undefined promise. He wanted to ask her to stay a little longer, but he once again reminded himself that she was here for work, not to discuss favorite movies, and the pause slipped away and the promise ebbed with it.

Once she'd left, he walked across to the large canvas and stared at those white and gray depths again. As much as he'd planned three life-size figures, he couldn't look at it now without imagining one small broken figure suspended in the middle of the icy expanse.

"Someone killed him."

He'd spoken aloud without realizing, the sound of his own voice startling against the silence of the studio.

There was no evidence to support a belief like that, nothing in Dorn's carefully hedged comments, nor in the journal that described the kind of friendship breakdown common to groups of students the world over. So there were some missing buttons, suggestive of a tussle—it meant nothing.

There was no reason to believe his father had been murdered, none at all, and yet he felt it in his core. Someone had fought with him, and whether by accident or design, they'd sent him to his death.

The thought took hold, even as Foster tried to counter it. A fight didn't signify a crime, and yet still he couldn't shake the idea that those missing buttons did signify more than a fight, and that at least one person in that old photograph knew more than they'd ever said about how Charles Treherne had died.

Eight

Forgot to take my journal with me! Just back from Admont Monastery in Austria. Most amazing library, and J's folks arranged for us to get special private access. Phenomenal. My life has gotten a whole lot more interesting thanks to P, no question about it. Oh, and something else to report. Had some really great conversations with L, at least when G wasn't around. Too soon to tell, I guess, but I think there's a real connection between us.

It was from near the front of the journal, and his mom and dad weren't a couple yet. There was something touching about seeing the early stages of infatuation committed to paper like this. And there was something almost magical about the survival of this journal deep inside the glacial ice, a time capsule emerging three decades after both Charlie and Lucy had died.

Even without dates for guidance, Foster knew that somewhere in the middle of this journal, his mother had fallen pregnant. Two months later, shortly after the final entry, his father would be dead, and nineteen months after that so would she.

Thankfully, his dad seemed to have been pretty coy about discussing the nature of his relationship with L in any detail. Foster hadn't read every entry yet, but all he could find so far were veiled references—"spent a few hours with L last night," "the time I get to be alone with L is the best of everything here," and then, nearer the end, "Problems for me and L," presumably referring to the problem that became Foster Treherne.

Maybe the rest of the journal was equally cryptic, rather than just being reticent about the subject of sex. Those troubling comments about G, or the suggestion of P starting out as a positive influence but ending as a negative one—for all Foster knew, they could conceal bitter conflicts within the group, the kind of feuds that might easily have spilled over into real violence.

He wondered too about the nature of the various expeditions described there, not those to the mountains but the others. What had been the group fascination with libraries and monasteries and burial sites? Was it just that they were all history students like Charles?

His dad, in one of the more flowery entries, had talked about them being engaged in a "noble endeavor," and Foster wondered what he'd meant by that. Had they been searching for something, or were they just a group of immature twentysomethings with overly vivid imaginations?

He guessed he would get answers to some of those questions the next day. Chris Hamblyn had been all too happy to agree to a meeting, even without the promise of an exclusive interview. He'd also passed on his sincere condolences, as if the death had only just occurred.

That was one of the hardest things for Foster to grasp. The thirty-two years probably seemed like no time at all to Charles and Lucy's former friends from Bologna. Or perhaps they remembered that time in the same way Foster did his own college years, simultaneously a lifetime ago and as fresh in the memory as the events of recent weeks.

It made Hamblyn or one of the other friends an ideal candidate for giving a eulogy, and certainly offered the best hope of having people attend the funeral who'd actually known Charles. But the stubborn unease in Foster's mind dictated that this meeting would be about more than funeral rites.

He wanted to know who they were, the names of the people in the picture, the identities behind the initials. He wanted to hear the stories behind the implied tensions that had become steadily worse as the journal progressed. Above all, he wanted to know who had loved his father, who had been angry with him, and just who these friends had really been.

Nine

Foster flew down to Rome midmorning. He'd arranged to meet Chris Hamblyn for lunch in the Hotel de Russie, but Natsuko called as Foster was checking in to say that Hamblyn had been delayed and was asking if they could meet for drinks instead.

So at three he walked out onto the sheltered terrace of the Stravinskij Bar. Hamblyn was already there. The wavy brown hair from the photograph had turned snowy white, though the style hadn't changed, and the boyish features were set heavy now, but he was instantly recognizable.

Hamblyn stood as Foster approached, recognizing him in turn, hardly surprising given that Hamblyn was a journalist and Foster a well-known artist. But as he reached the table, the older man held out a hand and said, "You look so much like Charlie—it's uncanny. Pleased to meet you, Foster."

"Likewise, thanks for agreeing to meet with me." Foster placed the envelope he was carrying on the table and they both sat down. Hamblyn already had a drink in front of him, what looked like a gin and tonic, and when the waiter approached, Foster said, "Could I get an Aperol Spritz, please."

"Certainly, Mr. Treherne."

As the waiter walked away again, Hamblyn made a show of looking impressed and said, "They recognize you? Or do you stay here a lot?"

"I've stayed here a few times, but . . . I think they're just professional." Even as he spoke, he noticed two ladies at a neighboring table looking over at him and maybe they *did* recognize him, because it was the kind of hotel that attracted the well-heeled minority who followed the art world. "You're the first person I've ever met who knew my dad—apart from his parents, of course."

"Really?" Hamblyn sipped at his drink and smiled warmly. "He was a lot of fun. It's been a tough couple of days for me since hearing the news. Brought back a lot of memories, things that seem like yesterday but . . . well, you know. And sorry, I'm sure it's been a lot tougher for you—"

"Not really. I didn't know him at all. It's almost like he's nothing to do with me. That's why I'm trying to find out more about him, his friends, things like that." Foster reached for the envelope and took out the copy of the photo Axel had printed off for him, the picture from the paper. "I was hoping you'd be able to tell me about the people in this photograph."

Hamblyn smiled as Foster placed it in front of him, even though it couldn't be new to him. He'd have seen it in his own paper's coverage, had maybe even supplied it to the *New York Times* himself.

"Your mom was a real beauty, and talented, too. No doubt that's where you get your artistic talent from."

Foster had never heard anything about her being artistic. He remembered seeing no mementoes of his mother's childhood, and certainly no youthful artwork. But then, his recollection of his English grandparents' home was that it resembled the house of a childless couple who'd adopted a baby in later life—if Lucy had ever left an imprint there, it had been erased long before Foster was old enough to be aware of it.

Chris Hamblyn responded to Foster's blank expression, saying, "You didn't know? Her course was researching Renaissance art, but she'd go off for the day and come back with the most incredible sketches she'd done of the various paintings she'd been to see. I'm no connoisseur and I was less of one back then, but she was a real natural."

"I had no idea."

Hamblyn pointed to the picture again, this time to the slim blonde woman standing in front of him. "This is Josefin. Josefin Widegren. We're still close, so I can put you in touch if you'd like. From Stockholm, but she's lived in Cap d'Antibes for the last twenty years or so." He pointed to the other woman, darker-haired, more buttoned-up in some way. "Marianne . . . What was her surname? It'll come back to me, though we never stayed in touch. And that's Giorgio." He pointed at the Italian-looking man in the white shirt and cravat. "I liked Giorgio, but we never stayed in touch either. I've no idea what happened to him. Of course, he was with your dad on that trip, though he didn't walk out with him that day, more's the pity."

Foster was absorbing as much of this onslaught of information as he could. Josefin Widegren was presumably the "J" whose parents had obtained special permission for the friends to visit the library in the Austrian monastery. Marianne was the "M" that appeared occasionally in the journal. And Giorgio was surely the "G" who'd started out so well but who'd become controlling and jealous, and he was the only one of the group who'd been with Foster's dad on the Handeck Glacier trip.

"Do you know why he didn't go out with my dad that day?"

The waiter arrived with Foster's drink before Hamblyn had the chance to answer.

Then Hamblyn raised his glass and said, "To your dad."

Foster raised his own glass and took a sip before putting it down again.

And Hamblyn nodded, frowning, before saying, "Giorgio had a heavy cold. He really shouldn't have gone on the trip at all, and I think he had planned to cancel, but then he realized everyone else had backed out for one reason or another and he saw your dad would be on his own, so he decided to go with him. But the cold got worse, and by that final day he just wasn't in any condition to go out."

A cold could be faked easily enough, or exaggerated, but Foster let it go and said, "My dad's journal was in his pack, wrapped in plastic so it's still in perfect condition. He refers to everyone by initials, but I wondered if you could help me with a few of them. Would you be H?"

Hamblyn smiled, looking immediately emotional, his eyes glistening. "Yes, I'd imagine that refers to me. They all called me Ham, partly because of my surname, partly because it was my first time in Italy and I couldn't get enough of Italian ham. Ham for Ham! Josefin still calls me that when we meet."

"What about P?"

"Man or woman?" Foster shrugged and Hamblyn said, "I don't remember anyone with that initial. Giorgio's surname is Pichler, but . . . Your dad mentions them alongside the rest of us?"

"He first mentions him—or her—after your trip to Livorno, then later mentions something about life being a lot more interesting thanks to P."

"Ah!" Hamblyn smiled, as if in response to an in-joke. "Our secret's out."

"I don't follow."

Hamblyn waved his hand at the photograph. "This is P, all of us, not one person but a society—an informal one at any rate. We were the Piranesi Society. It sounds pretentious now, and in truth I think I knew it was pretentious even then, but it was an adventure, a lot of fun, with an amazing group of friends."

Foster nodded, and resisted the urge to point out that Chris Hamblyn was only in touch with one of this "amazing group of friends" now, and couldn't even remember the second name of another.

"Named after the Italian artist?"

"No." Hamblyn was about to continue, but was distracted as a glamorous older woman approached the table and started talking to him enthusiastically in Italian. He stood, kissed her on both cheeks, and spoke back with a fluency that suggested he'd been here since his student days. The woman cast a few glances in Foster's direction, as if hinting that she was waiting to be introduced, but Hamblyn refused to take the bait, and after more dramatic kissing, she went on her way and Hamblyn sat down again. "Sorry about that. Where was I?"

"You were telling me about the Piranesi Society."

"Of course. You have to remember, we were a group of post-graduate history students in our mid-twenties. We weren't exactly hedonistic—the two passions we shared as a group were exploring ancient libraries, catacombs, monasteries, that kind of thing, and mountain sports, hiking and skiing mainly. This was the 1980s— that whole Indiana Jones vibe was really popular."

"So why Piranesi?"

"It's convoluted. Do you know much about Philipp von Stosch?"

"Nothing."

"He was a Prussian aristocrat, active in Rome and Florence in the first half of the eighteenth century—an antiquarian, a spy, but he also founded a Masonic Lodge in Florence that was thought to have turned corrupt, engaging in alchemy, Rosicrucian practices. You can imagine how that appealed to all of us. Stosch was an interesting character. Then Charlie discovered a little-known fact, that Stosch is buried in the Old English Cemetery in Livorno, a place that's closed to the public. We could have just arranged access, but we thought it might be more of an adventure if we did a midnight raid, so that's what we did, scaled the walls in the middle of the night and visited Stosch's tomb. We'd already become firm friends, already had these pretty esoteric shared interests, but that was the moment we became a society." He smiled to himself, presumably at the memories coming back to him in talking about that time. "I'm sure it sounds ludicrous to you, but really, it was so much fun."

"I still don't understand, why—"

"Of course. Why Piranesi? The reason Stosch's tomb is so little known is that it actually bears the name Piranesi. That kind of secret meaning, known only to us, it tied in with our admittedly childish beliefs that there were dark secrets and mysteries to be revealed in Europe's various libraries and ancient monuments. Like I said, it was that whole Indiana Jones thing, searching for lost knowledge."

Foster nodded, happy that he at least knew the identity of P. And it made sense in a way, that in the early days his dad had thought the Piranesi Society had made his life a lot more interesting, and yet by the end he was questioning whether it was doing good for any of them. Foster had often wondered the same about The New Painters, though probably not as much as his fellow former members had wondered about it.

"Did you ever find anything, any lost knowledge or hidden secrets?"

"No!" Hamblyn laughed, shaking his head. "We were kids."

"You were in your mid-twenties."

Hamblyn seemed to see that as affirmation rather than the contradiction Foster had intended. "Exactly!"

"The same age I was when I represented the USA at the Venice Biennale."

"Well, if you put it like that, sure, I guess some people mature faster than others."

"I didn't have a lot of choice."

"No, of course. And I'm sorry about that."

"It wasn't your fault." Foster sipped at his drink and Hamblyn followed suit with his. "My dad's journal seems to suggest things had turned sour by the end."

Hamblyn put his drink down again, looking puzzled. If it was an act, it was a good one.

"I wouldn't say they'd soured. You know how it is with things like this. In the early days it's all a heady rush, everyone's completely committed, but then other interests get in the way, other distractions, people drift apart."

Once again, Foster recognized this description as matching his experience with The New Painters.

"People fall out," he said.

"No, I wouldn't say that, either. I'm not suggesting there weren't occasional tensions or arguments over one thing or another, but no more so than in any group of close friends. There were some big characters. I mean, I remember Jo—Josefin—wasn't at all happy because I started dating an Italian science student and inevitably ended up spending a lot more time with her than I did with the rest of the group."

Hamblyn looked briefly at the photograph that was still on the table, and Foster caught a look in his eye, an immediate edginess, as if he'd suddenly seen something in that picture that unnerved him. Foster looked at it himself, but couldn't be sure what the older man had spotted there.

"Maybe I'm wrong. I just got the impression my dad had some issues, particularly with someone he refers to as G. I'm guessing that would be Giorgio?"

There was a pause, so brief as to be barely noticeable, before Hamblyn said, "Possibly. I thought Charlie and Giorgio got along fine, but they skied and hiked a lot together, so maybe what you're picking up on is just that—you know, the way two guys can irritate each other. They were great friends really. That's why Giorgio didn't want to let him down on that final trip."

"Could they have fought, come to blows? I mean, could that be the reason Giorgio didn't walk with him?"

As Foster spoke, Hamblyn looked more and more bemused, and said quickly, "No! I was talking about minor irritations, not violence. Neither of them was like that."

Yet somebody had torn the buttons from his dad's shirt.

"Were they romantic rivals?"

"I doubt it. Giorgio had plenty of girlfriends, but always Italian or German—he was from the German-speaking part of Italy, so he spoke both languages. I don't think he ever showed much interest in the girls in our group. He was always charming with them, but there was never any sense of him hitting on them."

Foster wasn't sure how that squared with his dad suggesting G was "borderline creepy" or that his constant presence was stopping him from befriending Lucy.

But then Hamblyn put Foster on the back foot, saying guardedly, "From the tone of your questions, I'm sensing you think something sinister was going on here, that maybe it played a part in your father's death. If that's the case, I hope I can assure you that your fears are completely without foundation."

"Actually, I was just trying to get a sense of my dad's state of mind on the day he died, trying to understand why he set out in bad weather on a hike he should have abandoned." He fixed his eyes on Hamblyn. "It hadn't occurred to me there might be something sinister—at least, not until you just mentioned it."

Hamblyn laughed. "Well, I set myself up for that one, didn't I? It was something other students, particularly other expat students, would often throw at us, and we kind of encouraged it at the time. But there were no weird rituals, nothing sinister. And I don't know what Charlie's state of mind was that day, but it didn't shock me at the time that he headed out like that. He was a lot of fun, but he had a reckless streak, and if he set out that day it wouldn't have been because he was despondent and suicidal, it would have been because . . . because that's the way he was. Your dad followed his own rules, and the world was a lot richer for having someone like that in it."

Foster nodded, accepting the comments as true. And it was telling in itself that Hamblyn thought Foster suspected a possible suicide, not murder. Listening to him talk, Foster was also struck again that Chris Hamblyn would be the ideal candidate to give a eulogy.

"I was wondering . . . The funeral will be in his hometown—Hopton, Connecticut—if you'd like to come."

There it was, another involuntary glance at the photograph, another hint of unease or even panic in Hamblyn's eyes. What was he seeing there? What could be so disturbing?

"I'd love to, of course. But if it's in the next two or three weeks, I'm just not gonna be able to get there. It looks like we've got elections coming here in Italy, and the migrant crisis is getting worse by the day . . . You know how it is."

Foster knew how it sounded, like someone latching on to the first excuse to avoid having to attend a funeral. That didn't mean Hamblyn was lying, of course. Whatever closeness there had been, maybe the passing of three decades had simply eroded it.

"Sure, I understand. Maybe your Swedish friend, if you have her details for me."

"Yes, of course. I'm certain she'd love to go if she can."

"I'd like to meet her even if she can't make the funeral. I didn't know either of my parents."

Hamblyn nodded, and said, "They'd have both been so proud."

It was the kind of platitude people said all the time, and it rang so obviously false in Foster's ears. Hamblyn had no idea what Foster's parents would have thought, because he had gone on living and they had not.

And as one doubt led to another, so Foster began to question everything he'd heard in the last half-hour, about how well they'd all gotten along, how there had been nothing sinister about the Piranesi Society, and how there was no reason to suspect his father's death was the result of anything more than a misplaced youthful recklessness.

Ten

Foster flew back to Berlin the next morning, but he was still dwelling on the conversation with Chris Hamblyn. It wasn't so much the things he'd said, but all the things Foster had sensed beneath the surface.

Foster's dad had been a lot of fun, to the point of being reckless, and a great person to be around. There apparently hadn't been any serious tensions in the group, and certainly not with Foster's dad. Nor had there been anything sinister about the Piranesi Society, despite what some people had thought at the time—and that old suspicion had been Hamblyn's excuse for his unsolicited defense of the society's activities.

But if they'd been so close, why couldn't Hamblyn even remember Marianne's surname, and why did he have no idea at all about what had happened to her or Giorgio Pichler? It suggested the group of friends had blown apart, much as The New Painters had.

In the case of The New Painters, Foster understood exactly why that had happened. One of them, Foster Treherne, had become instantly and fabulously successful, and the subsequent squabbles and recriminations had torn apart even those who should have been united in their resentment of Foster.

According to Hamblyn, no such feud had plagued the Piranesi Society. It had been, by his own definition, an outlet for youthful exuberance, and it had simply run its course. They'd never fallen out.

But twice during the brief conversation below the grand terraces of the Hotel de Russie, Chris Hamblyn had seen something in that group photograph, something that had rattled him. Foster was certain of it, and as soon as the plane had levelled out after leaving Ciampino Airport, he slipped the picture from the envelope and studied it, hoping to see what he was convinced Hamblyn had seen.

The first thing Foster noticed, though, from a purely artistic point of view, was the composition. It had clearly been taken by someone with no visual flair, and as a result, the six people in the photograph looked awkwardly framed. Foster couldn't quite work out why—maybe the individual poses, maybe the wrong people standing in the wrong places—but it was immediately apparent all the same.

Beyond that, there was nothing he could see about the people themselves that might be alarming or suggestive of some hidden secret. And they really did look as Hamblyn had portrayed them, a handful of twentysomethings who'd formed a close bond. Charlie and Lucy were on the other side of the frame, with Charlie on the far left and Lucy standing next to him. They were both trying to look aloof, even disdainful, but there was the trace of a smile on both faces, as if they were being playful and only just holding it together. Charlie had his hands in his pockets, and Lucy had her arm casually linked through his.

On the right, Hamblyn was standing a step higher than Josefin Widegren, a hand on her shoulder. He was smiling whereas she was laughing, in a way that suggested maybe he'd cracked some joke just before the picture was taken. Marianne, whose surname Hamblyn hadn't been able to remember, was standing on the same step as him, though she was some way shorter than him and there was a slight gap between them. Her eyes were raised in mock disapproval, as if she were ready to chastise him for whatever joke he'd just told.

Giorgio Pichler stood below her and to the left, almost bridging the gap between Josefin and Lucy. His head was partially turned and he seemed to be looking at Lucy, an enigmatic smile on his face. Was it the smile of a love rival? It was hard to say, but there was also a long road between being a love rival and a killer.

Yet there was no doubt at all in Foster's mind that Hamblyn had spotted something unusual in this picture. And maybe it would have been equally obvious to the other three surviving people captured there, but no matter how long Foster stared, he couldn't see what it was. There were no suspicious glances, no troubling body language, no hint of danger ahead.

And the more he looked at the photograph, the more he could imagine the appeal of this select little society. He imagined them as his dad had described them in the journal, lounging around in a candlelit chapel drinking red wine, or exploring the ancient texts in some labyrinthine monastic library. That was all visible in the faces in front of him—the allure, the romance—but he could see nothing darker.

He put the picture aside, leaned back, and closed his eyes, and though he didn't fall into a proper sleep, he only opened them again when the plane started to skip and vibrate a little heading across the Alps. He looked out of the window then, a clear view to the white peaks below, and couldn't help but think of all the other bodies waiting to emerge.

Professor Dorn had mentioned that such discoveries were becoming increasingly common, particularly later in the summer as the glaciers retreated a little more with each passing season. And in just about every case, the victims had fallen prey to bad weather or the wrong clothing or their own folly.

So why was Foster so convinced that something else had been at play here? Had Dorn planted the seed with his comments about a possible fight and about no one else being there that day? And had Hamblyn nurtured it, with his edgy glances at the photograph, with his vaguely unconvincing recollections?

Maybe it was because Foster had viewed the body himself. Maybe by staring into that partly mummified face, of a person long-dead who'd given him half his being, he'd been able to sense a truth that lay somewhere beyond forensics—traces of energy, like background radiation; an echo of his death preserved in the ice along with his hair and flesh.

Maybe, too, that same connection was behind the doubts that persisted about the group photograph. It wasn't even Hamblyn's nervous glances, but rather an instant subliminal reaction in Foster's own mind, convincing him that there was indeed something sinister concealed within that picture. He had only his own instinct to rely on, but if he was right, the truth of what had happened was somewhere there, hidden in the faces of the Piranesi Society.

Eleven

Foster was back at the studio early in the afternoon. Natsuko updated him on the funeral, which would take place in a little over a week's time. He noticed two letters then, sitting on the desk—or rather, he noticed the Comic Sans typeface.

Natsuko said, "The news seems to have gotten them excited. One came yesterday and another today."

He looked at them in turn. The first was more or less the usual, accusing him of being a fraud, promising him a "day of reckoning." The second was more interesting.

So they found a body. And you'll use it the way you've used everyone else. That's what frauds do.

He handed it back and said, "Send them across to Sigrid, I guess. But I don't think this is anything to worry about, just some failed artist who hates my success or some bitter person from my past."

"That sounds right to me. Can you think of anyone who might feel like that?"

"I can think of—"

He stopped short just in time, spotting Natsuko's sly smile. She knew all too well there were eleven other people who'd been in The New Painters who probably felt like that, and plenty more besides.

"Give me a break—I just flew back from Rome."

She shrugged and said, "How did it go?"

"Interesting. He said nice things about my dad, and about my mom—said she'd been quite a talented artist, you know, copies of the Renaissance paintings she was studying, that kind of thing."

Maja was walking past, heading toward her desk, but said, "That must be where you get it from."

Natsuko nodded. "Maja's right. A gift like yours, it has to come from somewhere." Almost protectively, she placed a hand over the two most recent letters, but that only made Foster take note of them all the more. "But it's good for you to hear about them from their friends."

"Yeah, I guess. He's too busy to come to the funeral, though. He gave me the number and address of the blonde woman in the photograph, so I'll call her." He looked around the office, not even sure what he was looking for. "Has Daniela Herrera been in touch?"

"Sure. There were some formalities to discuss, but I think it's all taken care of now."

He nodded, but stood still for a moment, lost, the way he often was when he first returned from a trip—though the dislocation seemed greater this time for some reason. Then he headed up to the empty apartment and put in a call to Josefin Widegren.

Her phone rang for a long time, so long that he kept expecting it to run on to voicemail, but the tone continued, persistent and high-pitched. And when she answered, it took a moment for Foster to realize she'd spoken, a few abrupt words, possibly in French, but too quick for him to understand.

"Miss Widegren?"

There was a pause of a few seconds before she said, suspiciously, "Yes, who is this?"

"My name's Foster Treherne, I—"

She laughed, interrupting him, and her tone was completely different as she said, "Ah, so it's true! Ham warned me you'd be in touch. I didn't think you'd take the trouble to do it yourself."

"Excuse me?"

"I assumed I'd be hearing from some assistant or PR person."

"Oh, I see. Well, no, I wanted to call in person. After all, you were a friend of my parents."

There was another pause—too long, thought Foster, just to formulate a response to such a simple statement—before she said, "Yes, I was."

"So, my father's funeral is going to be a week on Friday, and naturally, you'd be very welcome if you were free to come."

"Where will it be?"

"In Hopton, Connecticut. It's where he grew up."

She'd started speaking even as Foster was still answering, saying, "In the USA? Then I'm sorry to tell you it's out of the question. I haven't flown in an airplane for over five years. None of us should be flying, so it's my little stand, you know, for the environment."

"Sure, I understand that." He was stung on his dad's behalf, but then, he didn't know just how strongly she felt about limiting her carbon footprint. "Alternatively, would it be possible for me to visit with you at some point before then? I'm just trying to meet some of the people who knew him, who knew both of them."

"I'd be delighted. Do you have some paper?"

"Paper?"

"To write down my address."

"Oh, I have it already. Chris Hamblyn gave it to me."

"Of course he did."

She laughed again, and Foster thought of the way she was laughing in the photograph. He needed to make her laugh like that, to remind her of the good times she'd shared with Hamblyn and the others. And maybe if he succeeded in making her nostalgic, she'd open up about the rest of it, too.

But at the same time, Foster thought of all the writers and journalists who'd interviewed him over the last decade, how they'd probably strategized in a similar way, hoping he'd open up about The New Painters or about his own childhood. It only highlighted his problem now, because if someone didn't want to talk, it was hard to lure them into doing so.

Twelve

Josefin Widegren would almost certainly guess that Foster had flown in from Berlin, though he wouldn't tell her it was by private jet into Cannes Mandelieu rather than a scheduled flight into Nice. He'd at least opted out of a helicopter transfer, but after forty minutes in crawling traffic out to the Cap, he was beginning to regret that.

Her property was concealed from the road, but beyond the gate it was a jumble of modernist glass boxes set in its own botanical gardens, surrounded by towering umbrella pines.

As he got out of the car, he could see her drifting through the glass maze of the interior, heading toward him. She was still blonde, still looked slim, but was wearing a blue-and-gold embroidered kaftan that gave the impression of someone who'd been young in the 1960s, not the 1980s.

She opened the door and stepped out, smiling. Up close he could see her skin was tanned and full of fine wrinkles, the face of a blonde who'd spent her life in the sun.

"You look uncannily like your father. Though your coloring is more from Lucy."

Given the hippie aesthetic and the modernist house, he was surprised when she held out her hand and gave him an oddly formal handshake.

"Thanks for agreeing to see me."

"It's the least I could do." She looked down at the envelope in his hand, then back up at Foster. "Why don't you walk around the house to the terrace, and I'll bring out the drinks."

"Sure."

She turned and walked back inside, closing the glass door behind her. Foster turned to the driver, who was standing beside the car—Josefin had apparently failed to notice him.

"I'll try not to keep you too long."

The driver shrugged. "Don't worry, sir, I have a drink in the car." He looked at the house. "Nice place she has here."

Foster nodded and walked around the building, conscious of the feel of the Mediterranean very close by, even though it wasn't visible beyond the greenery. The terrace overlooked a large pool, the water pristine, sparkling pale blue.

An ornate gazebo provided shade for the table and chairs beneath it. Foster walked toward it at the same time as she emerged from the back of the house carrying a tray with a jug of something and glasses.

"Please sit down. Do you like iced tea?"

"Yes. Thanks."

They sat and she poured him a drink. He sipped it, found it packed with too much mint, and put the glass back on the table.

"I don't follow art very much, but I've seen how well your career has been these last ten years. That would have made Lucy very happy."

Hamblyn had told Foster that she'd lived in Antibes for twenty years, but when she spoke English she still had the unmistakably musical lilt of a native Swedish speaker.

"I hope so. I like to think it would have made both of them happy." He liked to think no such thing, and hadn't ever given much thought to how either parent might have viewed his art

70

career—they'd opted out too long ago to be worthy of consideration on that score. He'd said it more to gauge her reaction, but Josefin smiled politely, said nothing, and took a sip of her iced tea. "It's a beautiful house you have here."

She looked out beyond the pool to the gardens rather than at the house behind her, and said, "Yes, I've been very lucky. I built it with my ex-husband. We set up an internet company and sold it about a year before the dot-com crash at the turn of the century. It's a sign of how amicable our divorce was that he didn't fight me for this place."

"Do you have children, Josefin?"

"Please, call me Jo. I have a son. He's studying marine science in California." She smiled, and for the first time since he'd arrived, there seemed some real warmth in it. "But you haven't come here to talk about such things. Ham told me. You want to ask about us, about the Piranesi Society."

Something about the way she spoke suggested that this society had meant a lot to them, more than The New Painters had ever meant to him and the others. He wasn't sure why, but her tone gave him the impression of a society that was still current rather than three decades in the past, something for which they still felt ownership.

"Yes, I do. Chris Hamblyn told me it was named after a tomb in a closed cemetery, the tomb of Philipp von Stosch."

"That was your dad's idea! Oh yes, Charlie was so great at coming up with madcap adventures like that."

"But you went along with it?"

"Of course!" She looked briefly lost in the memory. "We went there at night! It's behind quite an ordinary apartment block, this remarkable little walled cemetery, almost entirely overgrown. Locked, of course. We climbed over the gate, which wasn't so easy—I think it was three or four meters—and then we searched with pocket flashlights until we found the von Stosch tomb. I'm sure there was no danger, but it *felt* dangerous. Thrilling, actually."

Listening to her, seeing how transported she was just by the telling of it, Foster once again felt the gnawing envy he'd experienced when first reading his father's journal. Sneaking into a closed cemetery at night was a ridiculous thing to do, something Foster and his friends at college would have considered too juvenile for words, and yet hearing about it now only made him think he and his social circle had been nowhere near juvenile enough.

"So what happened once you found the tomb—you took selfies and left?"

He'd been so transported that he'd momentarily forgotten how long ago this was, but before he had the chance to correct himself, Josefin laughed and said, "Selfies! This was before cellphones, let alone smartphones with cameras. But we did something much better. Giorgio brought a bottle of pine schnapps and little shot glasses. We raised a toast to von Stosch. Then we cut our fingers and dripped blood onto the tombstone." She smiled wistfully. "It all seems so silly now, but we genuinely believed we were engaged in some great search for arcane knowledge. We were committed. Yes. And we were deadly serious about the society."

Deadly serious.

Foster said, "Chris Hamblyn told me it was set up after that visit."

"Not *after*, it was right there and then. We were already like a little society—our beliefs and interests were all so closely aligned—but it was as we stood by von Stosch's tomb, drinking more schnapps, that we decided to make it a real society."

"And the name?"

"That was . . . Giorgio's idea, I think." Her hesitation didn't seem like an attempt at recalling whose idea it had been—the whole evening appeared to be incredibly fresh in her mind—but rather as if she'd been about to say one name but had decided to change it to another. But why? Why would she want to conceal whose idea it had been? "Lucy had suggested naming it after von Stosch himself. But Giorgio, he reminded us that von Stosch was still a controversial figure, that we had to think about our future careers. A little overblown, I think, but when he suggested Piranesi, and how it would be like a secret code, we all loved the idea. So it became the Piranesi Society."

Foster took the photograph out of the envelope and handed it to her, saying, "I was hoping you could help me identify one or two of the people in this."

He studied her face carefully as she caught sight of the picture, but there was nothing of Hamblyn's alarm. Instead, she beamed.

"And there we are! The Piranesi Society. We all look so *young*." With one finger she caressed Lucy's face, a brief flicker of sadness crossing her features. "But surely you know most of these people now."

"The other woman. Chris Hamblyn could remember her first name, but not her surname."

Josefin shook her head in mock disbelief, and said, "Ham's losing his memory. Marianne Arthur. She doesn't look it here—so prim and proper—but she was a riot."

"Did you keep in touch?"

"For a little while. But again, this is before the internet and Facebook and . . . She was from New York, old money—I expect she married someone equally blue-blooded."

"And the Italian man." Foster had googled the name Giorgio Pichler, but hadn't spotted anyone who looked like a match. "Do you know what happened to him?"

"Giorgio!" She looked at the photograph again, smiling. "No, I don't know what happened to him, but he was lovely. We had a little affair, Giorgio and I, only for a month or two. I had such an irrational fear of losing him as a friend that I asked him if we could stop, and he agreed. That might sound strange, but he was so easygoing."

Foster nodded, wondering why an easygoing guy would suggest giving their society a secret name in case the association with von Stosch damaged their future careers. He also recalled Hamblyn saying that Giorgio had only dated Italian and German girls. Maybe it was all part of a coordinated effort by Chris Hamblyn and Jo Widegren to portray Giorgio as someone who'd never get into a fight.

"Did he have any involvement with either of the other two girls?"

"Sleep with them, you mean? No." She laughed. "We weren't *that* kind of society. No, it was just him and me, and now that I'm older, I do wonder sometimes what might have happened if I hadn't lost my nerve. I wouldn't be living here, of course. I'd probably be living in the Dolomites with him."

"I thought you didn't know what happened to him."

She stared at Foster, as if reassessing him.

"Your father was very sharp-witted." It sounded like an accusation. "I don't know what happened to Giorgio, but he was from the Dolomites, South Tyrol, and he loved it there. I'm positive it's where he would have settled. More iced tea?"

She pointedly looked at Foster's barely touched glass. He leaned forward and took a couple of hefty gulps, before holding out the glass to her for a refill.

"Thanks. It's . . . very minty."

"Good for the digestive system."

He took another dutiful sip, then put the glass down again and said, "If I sound confused or doubtful in some way, it's only because you were all so close, a tight group of friends, and yet apparently, you just splintered apart, and not over time, but almost immediately."

"It's not so odd. When I look back now, I think it was a strange time to be young. The future was so close, you could . . . almost feel it. But it hadn't arrived yet. As I said to you, no internet, no cellphones, and sure, within a few years, there they were, but we had already gone our separate ways to separate countries. I imagine you've never written a letter in your life, but that was how we kept in touch to begin with, writing letters. And of course, two of our group died. Nothing would ever be the same after that."

The mention of letters briefly made Foster think of the Comic Sans letters arriving regularly at his studio in Berlin, but he was brought back to the here and now by the comment about the deaths of his parents and their impact on the group. He'd never been in a similar situation himself, but he would have imagined something like that might have brought the remaining members of the group closer together rather than causing them to scatter.

"What were they like, my parents?"

"Your father was a lot of fun, exciting, spontaneous. Lucy . . . I would describe her as playful rather than fun. She was a quiet person, studious, liked to be alone. You know? She was lost in her own thoughts a lot of the time. She was naive in some ways, too, and . . . I'm not sure, but I wasn't so surprised when I heard about her illness, or about her suicide. It was a weakness I think I saw in her from the beginning without really knowing it."

It was strange to hear her talk like this, entirely positive about his dad, but her comments about his mother laced with implied criticism, in the tone as much as in the words themselves. And yet when she'd first seen the photograph, she'd caressed Lucy's face in what had appeared an almost involuntary act of affection.

"Were they together long?"

75

"They were always close. We were all close. It was an intense friendship between us. But . . . I wouldn't say there was ever anything formal between Charlie and Lucy, just . . . well, you know how it is."

"I guess I do." He had wondered, after reading the journal, if they'd ever officially become a couple, if they'd even had time to think about it seriously before the pregnancy changed everything.

He made another attempt on the drink, but found it no more palatable.

Josefin sipped at hers, too, then said, "Were they able to determine the cause of death? With Charlie, I mean."

She'd made it sound as casual as possible, but it struck Foster that they were closing in on Josefin's reason for agreeing to see him. He wished now that he could have listened in on the phone conversation that had obviously taken place between Chris Hamblyn and Jo following Foster's trip to Rome.

"Not with any certainty. It's clear that he fell and sustained multiple injuries, including one to the back of the head which was probably the fatal blow, but . . ." He left the pause hanging there, with the implication that he knew a lot more than he was saying. "It's impossible to be precise."

"I see. Yes, it must be difficult, after so long."

Was there a hint of nervousness in her now? More importantly, there was no expression of sorrow or empathy, to the extent that Foster wondered if Josefin had actually liked his father at all. She'd told him how seriously they'd taken the society, whereas Charlie had been spontaneous, reckless—had he tired of it and left them feeling he'd betrayed them in some way? That seemed absurd, but so did dripping blood onto a tomb in a closed cemetery.

"Why was my father alone that day?"

Puzzled, Josefin said, "Giorgio was unwell."

"Then let me put it another way. Why were he and Giorgio alone? Why weren't the rest of you there?"

"It wasn't meant to be a Piranesi trip." She shrugged. "He and Giorgio often went off together."

"Charlie's journal says everyone was meant to be going."

There was a pause, during which Foster could hear a speedboat bouncing across the waves, sounding very close to where they were sitting.

Finally, she said, "Ham told me you'd found his journal. What does it say?"

"He says that everyone had originally planned to be on that trip, but you'd all dropped out. And he questions whether the Piranesi Society might actually have been bad for all of you."

Josefin nodded, but she also looked relieved, he thought, as if she'd feared some greater revelation from this long-lost journal. What were they afraid of? What did they think Charlie Treherne might have recorded in his private notes?

"Yes, things were . . . falling apart. When I look back now I think it's natural, an intense friendship that couldn't last, but still something beautiful while it did last. I never kept a diary, but if I had, perhaps I would have expressed the same view as your father at the time. It's like a relationship—you can never assess it properly just as it's ending. Later, you look back and think of the good times, and you remember only the love."

Foster nodded. Josefin Widegren said all the right things, but he didn't detect any real retrospective love for his father, and more than ever, he felt both she and Chris Hamblyn were covering something up, or else fearful that something would be exposed along with the reemergence of Charlie's body.

He thought of his father lying on that table in Bern, and then he thought of the glacial canvas back in the studio, once again imagining a small isolated body lost in the middle of it. Foster had never known him, yet he was convinced he felt more sorrow for the young man who'd died up on that glacier than Charlie's own friends did.

Charlie Treherne had been wronged, Foster was increasingly certain of it. And in some way he couldn't quite determine, the two friends he'd met were trying to ensure that Foster would never get to the truth.

Three decades on, his father's closest friends at the time of his death were hiding something, and the sense of loss they expressed was so superficial that they weren't even willing to attend the funeral. Maybe Foster hadn't known him at all, but he was absolutely convinced Charlie Treherne deserved more than that.

NEW ART PERIODICAL—ISSUE #8, FALL 2016

KM: You don't seem to have many friendships in the art world. Is that a conscious decision?

FT: Painting isn't a collaborative art form. Like most artists, I spend a big part of the day alone.

KM: Sure, but here in New York there are plenty of art events, a vibrant community of artists. You just seem a little outside of all that.

FT: It's not intentional.

KM: But you have to accept it follows a pattern?

FT: I don't follow.

KM: Well, after your initial success, didn't you cut yourself off from your former friends in The New Painters, even your girlfriend at the time?

FT: I wouldn't say I cut myself off. Not all of them went on to have careers, and even those who did . . . It's difficult. People assume I dropped my friends because I got famous, but they don't look at how your old friends change in their own behavior toward you.

KM: Even your girlfriend?

FT: No. Look, it was a long time ago.

KM: Only six years.

FT: Okay. It feels like a long time ago, and friendships don't last forever. Life moves on.

Thirteen

The car had just turned off I-95 at Norwalk when Claudia said, "No family at all?"

It was as if it had only just sunken in, now that they were getting farther from New York and the world she knew.

"No family at all. It's possible we'll be the only mourners."

"Well, that's insane."

Foster laughed. "Claudia, when I have to bring my gallerist with me, I think you're safe to assume it's not going to be the best-attended funeral."

"I consider it a privilege to come with you." She waited a moment before adding, "You know I'm Jewish?"

"And?"

"It's an Episcopal church, isn't it? It would be good to know how I'm meant to address . . . you know, like, the guy who's doing it."

"Well, the guy is called Rose, and she's a priest, I guess, or a rector. But you can call her Rose. I spoke with her briefly last night, and Natsuko's been in touch a few times. I don't think we need to worry about causing offense."

"Good, particularly if we're the only mourners." Claudia's phone buzzed and she looked at it but put it away again. "Mind if I swing by the studio tomorrow?"

"Not at all."

He knew what she wanted. Claudia was fully aware that he hadn't painted anything in the studio in Tribeca for over two years, but she also knew that there were a whole bunch of completed or near-completed paintings stored there. Each time he was in town, she'd persuade him to release one or two of them for a buyer who was "absolutely desperate."

"I have to warn you, though, I looked through all my canvases last night and I'm not happy with what I was painting back then. I've told Benny to destroy them."

"You shouldn't try to be amusing, Foster. You're not very good at it and it doesn't suit you."

He looked at her and laughed, and in the end she begrudged a laugh too, then told him about the buyer—a hedge-fund manager who already had two of Foster's pieces. They talked business more or less all the way to Hopton, and when they pulled up outside the church, Claudia looked as surprised as if they'd teleported there.

"Oh, we're here? What a pretty church. And what a pretty town. I had no idea."

"About Connecticut?"

"Stop it."

Foster had never been here before and yet it looked familiar somehow, a white church set on a leafy road with large white clapboard houses here and there along it. It reminded him of Bennington and the other parts of New England he'd come to know during his childhood.

There were plenty of cars and vans in the parking lot, but nobody around outside, despite a clear blue sky and a pleasant early-summer warmth in the air. Once they got inside the church, all became clear, and Foster's vision of a desolate funeral service with two mourners disappeared entirely.

It looked like there were a handful of curious locals, but they were massively outnumbered by press and by art junkies, people who'd probably come along out of ghoulish curiosity and to get a glimpse of Foster himself. A handful of flashes popped as smartphones were used to take pictures of him.

As they walked up the aisle, a woman at the end of one of the pews stood and turned to meet him. She was wearing what he could only think of as a fancy-dress version of funeral attire, including a hat and a black veil covering her face. She looked so much the part that Foster briefly wondered if he'd overlooked some relative he hadn't known about.

But then she held up her phone with the internationally recognized body language of "could I get a selfie?"

Claudia stepped in front of Foster and said, "Have you no shame! This is a funeral service. Now I suggest you take your seat or take your leave."

The woman visibly withered in front of Claudia's gaze and sat down again, her head bowed. Claudia turned, linked a protective arm in Foster's, and walked him the rest of the way to the first pew. The casket was there in front of them, and Foster felt an irrational urge to open it, to see if his father still looked as he had in Bern or if the morticians had attempted some cosmetic improvements.

Foster and Claudia sat down on the otherwise empty pew, but stood again immediately as the Reverend Rose came out to talk to him.

"Foster, welcome. I'm Rose." She smiled. She was probably only the same age as him, but looked like a thirty-one-year-old from an earlier generation—pretty in a homey, bake-sale kind of way. "It's so good to have you here in our church to celebrate your father's life."

"Thanks," said Foster, even as he was wondering how much of a celebration it could be.

There was no one here who'd known his dad, no one who'd loved him. Foster could imagine how this church might have looked if the young Charlie Treherne had been found right away—the relatives and family friends, a good number of his high school and Yale cohorts, maybe even the guilt-ridden fellow members of the Piranesi Society—and it felt fundamentally wrong that the intervening decades had robbed him of that proper send-off.

As if to prove that point, Rose smiled sympathetically and said, "Are you still certain you'd prefer no eulogy?"

"I am. I didn't know him. And no disrespect, but even if I had, I'm not certain I'd want to share my memories of him with this congregation."

She smiled, an expression that was sympathetic but noncommittal, and said, "I understand. Well, let's begin." She moved on and turned to face the congregation Foster had just implicitly bad-mouthed, and said cheerily, "Welcome! Please stand so that we can sing our first hymn, 'The Lord is my Shepherd'—he maketh me to lie down in green pastures: he leadeth me beside the still waters."

They all stood as the organ bellowed into life above them.

The service was short, the burial shorter. Some of the black-clad attendees hovered afterward as if expecting to be invited to a reception, and there were disappointed faces among them as Foster and Claudia headed back to their waiting car.

No one but the Reverend Rose and Claudia had spoken to Foster as of yet, not even to offer condolences, but as the driver opened the door for them, a journalist stepped from the crowd.

"Foster, it must have been strange and upsetting to have your father's body discovered after so long?"

Foster turned, spotting the journalistic ruse of asking a leading question, so that if he even nodded it would become "Foster Treherne agreed it had been strange and upsetting . . ."

Instead, he looked at the man in the well-worn black suit and said, "I have no comment to make at this time, but thank you for coming."

Another journalist looked ready to fire a question at him, but someone in the crowd shouted, "We love you, Foster!" and a few more joined in. He raised his hand in an appreciative wave and climbed into the car after Claudia.

Neither of them spoke until they were headed back out of Hopton, and then Claudia said, "That was nice, not as bad as it might have been. You okay?"

"Yeah, I think so." He looked out at the last of the well-appointed houses on the outer edges of town. For all he knew, one of them was the home his father had grown up in, the same one into which Foster's grandparents had resolutely refused to invite him, the same house he'd sold without even seeing a photograph of it. "It's weird that this town should have meant so much to me and yet I've never been here before and probably won't ever come again."

"Yes, it must be strange." She glanced out herself, and was facing the window as she said, "It's so pretty it makes me feel nauseous." Foster laughed and she turned and shrugged, smiling too, then her eyes opened wide. "I completely forgot! I didn't know Marianne Tolman was a friend of your father! In fact, why wasn't *she* here? Maybe she didn't know about it, though I find that highly unlikely."

"Claudia, *what* are you talking about?"

"I saw that picture they had in the *Times* and I spotted her right away. Obviously, she's a lot younger in the picture, but no mistaking it's her, and you know, I don't think she's had a single bit of work done. Good bone structure."

Foster was catching up and said, "Marianne Tolman? I assume you mean the wife of the internet guy?"

"Fintech, to be precise. But yes, Gregory Tolman! Marianne was his first wife. They both remarried, but she kept the name because of the children. She's an avid collector. She even has a couple of yours."

"Does she?"

Foster thought back to the picture. Marianne Arthur. Was that why Hamblyn hadn't been able to remember her name, because he thought of her now only by her more famous married name? But then, both Hamblyn and Josefin Widegren had expressed ignorance of what had happened to her subsequently, which seemed unlikely given one of them was a journalist and the other had owned an internet company.

"Could I meet her while I'm in town?"

"You want me to set something up?"

"Sure."

"Okay, I'll get on it as soon as I'm back."

"Thanks."

In many ways, Marianne Arthur had seemed like the least interesting person in that group photo—attractive without being striking, stylish without being ostentatious—and if the two people Foster had already met had revealed simply that she'd gone on to marry the billionaire tech pioneer Gregory Tolman, he'd have thought nothing of it.

There was no question in Foster's mind that both Hamblyn and Josefin had to have known what had become of her, which meant they'd had a reason for concealing that particular truth from him. Whatever their intentions had been, their pointless secrecy had transformed Marianne Arthur from being the least interesting person in that photograph to possibly the most interesting.

Fourteen

The Tribeca studio was part of an old warehouse. It was a similar setup to his Berlin studio, with a large workspace, storage, an office, and a loft apartment above. But this being New York, it wasn't quite as big, and although he liked coming back here and felt a certain nostalgia for the place, he knew why he'd moved on. He'd felt too hemmed in—by the building, by the neighborhood, by the New York art scene.

The funeral had been a reminder of that, too. Occasionally in Berlin, someone would recognize him and ask for a selfie, usually an American or Japanese tourist, but on the whole, he was anonymous there. The funeral had been a flashback to what it had been like for a while living here—Foster wasn't famous in absolute terms, but he was famous enough among a certain kind of person, and a lot of those people lived in New York.

Benny wasn't at his desk yet when Foster walked through the office the next morning and into the studio space. That wasn't unusual—he didn't come in until around eleven. In truth, Foster didn't need an assistant here at all, but if he let Benny go he'd have to accept that he no longer needed this studio either, and he still had a sentimental attachment to it.

The studio itself was almost bare. An old desk with an office chair was against the wall to one side, and a paint-spattered couch, just like the one in Berlin, sat in the middle of the floor, but there were no longer any canvases propped against the walls, no paints or materials on trestle tables and shelves. Even the distinctive smell of paint had been reduced to the faintest aroma.

He'd stayed in London for a year or two after the breakthrough with The New Painters, but then he'd yielded to the siren call of this city, and his time in this studio had coincided with his ascent into the highest reaches of the art establishment. The invitations, the accolades, the attention—all had come his way during his first couple of years here.

He slid open the double-height door into the storeroom and switched on the lights. There were maybe forty or fifty paintings in here, all shelved on rollers in two long rows. He moved along first one row, then the other, pulling the paintings clear, dismissing most before they were fully visible, knowing that he still considered them unfinished or, worse, unsatisfactory.

In the end he selected five and slowly worked to move them out into the studio, where he leaned them against the walls. One of them was from what had become known as his *Brueghel* series— highly populated canvases, but each with one strikingly solitary figure—and this was the only one in that series not to have sold, because he'd continued to work on it long after the original show. He was giving Claudia and her prospective buyer a choice, but he was confident this was the painting they'd choose.

Once he was done he went back through to the office and brewed a pot of coffee. He poured a cup, then pulled open the desk drawer and took out the sketch pad Benny kept there. Benny was a sculptor, most of his work exploring what he called his "Transatlantic Heritage," the troubled transition usually reduced to a single hyphen in the word "African-American." He was good, too, but despite admiring words after his first show, the sales and commissions hadn't really followed.

Benny came in as Foster was looking, and said, "Hey Foster, sorry if I'm late."

"You're not late. Hope you don't mind."

Benny looked at the open sketchbook and shook his head. "What do you think?"

"Some of these look great. They've moved on."

"I like to think so."

"How many of these have you made?"

"Of those? None. I got kicked out of my studio—it's getting redeveloped as upscale apartments."

Benny poured himself a coffee. He was only six years younger than Foster, which made it difficult to advise him, to tell him he was still young, that he'd get his breakthrough, because Foster's had come much earlier than that, and plenty of great artists never got their due while plenty of average ones did.

As if to back up that lack of fairness, he'd had an email from Natsuko early that morning, saying only: *Two more today*. She didn't even need to spell it out. There'd been one or two of the Comic Sans notes every day for the last week, suggesting the news story about Foster's father had spurred an extra surge of resentment in the letter writer.

"What have you done with your equipment?"

"In a storage locker, but don't worry, I'll figure something out."

Foster doubted whether Benny would figure anything out, because the odds were stacked against most artists, and a piece of bad luck like losing studio space could prove the fatal blow for a lot of careers. Benny almost seemed to have the air about him of someone who knew he was going nowhere, that the game was up.

Foster thought of some of The New Painters, and wondered how long they'd persevered before they'd accepted it wasn't going to happen. Foster couldn't imagine ever giving up himself, but that self-belief had never been tested.

"Benny, you must know I don't really need an assistant in New York. I haven't needed one for two or three years now. I'm paying you to work for an hour or two a day, work that the crew in Berlin could do anyway." He saw Benny's expression collapsing, thinking he was about to be let go, and Foster realized too late that that was how it sounded, so he put his hand up to stop Benny from pleading for his job. "Relax, I'm not firing you. I need to keep the storage space, and I wanna keep this place, but it's about time I was honest with myself and accepted I'll never use this studio again. So *you* use it. You can still spend an hour a day doing my stuff, and the rest of the time, you can make your art."

"Foster, I'm grateful, really I am, but there's no way I could afford—"

"The rent? Did I say I wanted you to rent it from me? Benny, you'd be doing me a favor. This place needs to be used. So, like I said, as long as you don't use the storeroom, it's yours to do with as you like. I want you to use it."

Benny shook his head—not a rejection, but in disbelief that someone was willing to do this for him. Foster, on the other hand, couldn't believe it hadn't occurred to him to suggest it before now. He'd had plenty of his own lucky breaks, so what did it cost him to give a little of that good fortune to someone else?

"Seriously, man, you don't know what this means to me." Benny came over, gave Foster a quick hug, and when he backed away, Foster could see his eyes were moist with tears, a suggestion of just how little faith he'd had in finding a solution, or in getting anywhere at all with his career.

"I'm glad. You can arrange the details with my New York assistant." Benny laughed at that, and Foster added, "And while we're at it, that Tyler guy isn't doing you any favors. You should get Claudia to take you on."

"Easier said than done."

Foster picked up the sketch pad, pulled a few of the leaves free, and spread them casually on the table in the reception area, then checked his watch.

"Just leave the sketches there. She'll be here in about twenty minutes. Give me a call upstairs once she arrives."

"Sure thing, Foster."

He went back up to the apartment, though he might as well have offered that to Benny too. It no longer felt even remotely like a home, and in truth, it wasn't a convenient location for his increasingly infrequent trips to the city—he'd have been better staying at a hotel in Midtown.

Still, when Benny called him, he waited ten minutes before going down, and sure enough, by the time he got there, Claudia had spotted the sketches and was listening in earnest as Benny explained his vision.

As Foster joined them, he pretended to notice the sketches and said, "Can't wait to see these, Benny." Then he turned to Claudia and added, "Did he tell you the good news? I'm letting him have the studio as a workspace."

She nodded, apparently intrigued as much by Foster's gesture as by Benny's art, and said, "We're having lunch next week, aren't we, Benny?"

"Sure, that'd be great."

Foster said, "Why not, yeah, you two would work well together." He turned to Claudia then. "Wanna look at some paintings?"

She smiled and they walked through to the studio. She didn't speak for a full fifteen minutes, just moved from painting to painting, took a few pictures, used a measure to check dimensions which she tapped into her phone. She was clearly making every attempt to be open-minded, and if he'd let her, she'd have taken all of them and easily found buyers for the other four, but she knew how reluctant he was to flood the market.

"So you're finally ready to sell the last of the *Brueghel* series paintings."

"I think it's ready."

"It's more than ready." She took a few more pictures of just that one canvas. "I've made a decision. I'm not telling him about the others, just this one. I know he'll want it more than anything." She smiled and produced a satisfied sigh, but then the smile fell away and she said, "Oh, I forgot to mention, I spoke to Marianne Tolman. She, um . . . she doesn't want to see you."

"Did she say why?" Even as he asked the question, he wasn't entirely surprised at the refusal, and wasn't sure why, except for his belief that they were all trying to cover something up.

"Oh, she'd find it too upsetting, it's all in the past, she's too busy, yadda yadda yadda."

"Can you fire her details across to me? Maybe if I call her myself she'll be different."

"Might work, personal touch. You know, I don't know her very well, but it isn't at all like her. She's a classy lady. Unless, of course, she really didn't like your old man."

Foster smiled. His "old man" had never aged past twenty-five.

"She bought a couple of my paintings, so she can't have held that much of a grudge. Anyway, I'm meeting Abi for lunch, but I'll call her and see if I can go over this afternoon."

"Great idea. Give Abi my love." Claudia looked at her watch. "And now I have to go."

He saw her out before having Benny help to return the canvases to the storeroom. Then he walked the couple of blocks to the restaurant where he'd arranged to meet Abigail. He was on time—in her former career as Foster's nanny, punctuality had been one of the many basics of good manners she'd instilled in him—but she was there already, sitting at the table in the window.

Foster raised his hand in a wave as soon as he saw her, and felt the familiar swelling of his heart. He knew that he was incomplete, that the things missing from his childhood were manifest in the person he was today, but the extent to which he'd grown into a fully functioning adult at all was entirely due to the love and support this woman had given him through the first decade of his life.

Abi was in her fifties now, but she still looked young, as if he were catching her up. She stood to greet him and he hugged her and held on to her for a second, then she held him at a distance as if assessing him, a proud smile on her face.

"You'll always be my little boy."

He nodded, and they sat down and spent the next twenty minutes catching up, talking about her daughters—one starting at Columbia in the fall, the other coming to the end of her junior year of high school—about whether he'd yet found a new girlfriend or if there might be any hope of him getting back with Nele.

It was only after all that was taken care of and their food had arrived that Abi said, "And how are you dealing with your dad being found?"

"Okay, I guess. It's strange. His journal was in his backpack, so in a way I feel like I'm getting to know him now. And seeing the body—"

"Oh my goodness, Foster! You viewed the body?"

He nodded. "I didn't think it would trouble me, what with not having known him, but . . . I'm not sure how to explain it. It's a mummified body, so it doesn't look great—he had no ears—but you could still see it was a young man, younger than me. His hair, his face, there was still enough there to know who he'd been."

He considered telling her something about the Piranesi Society, about his suspicion that the surviving members were concealing something about the way his father had died, about his suspicion that Charlie Treherne had not died entirely by accident on that glacier. But he held back, conscious of how obsessive and fantastical it would sound. Sitting with Abi, he even began to question if he might be reading too much into everything.

"I imagine it'll take a while for me to come to terms with it. When I was little I always thought he'd come back."

She nodded, as if to remind him that she recalled those things as well as he did, and maybe better.

"I remember you talking to a friend once when you were about six, and you told him your dad was lost in *Swaziland*! But even then, you were adamant he'd come back."

"I guess he did, in the end. It kind of feels like he's coming back a little more with each new thing I find out about him."

The waiter came to their table and picked up the wine bottle to refill their glasses, but Abi refused with a quick hand gesture that for some reason reminded Foster of Daniela Herrera.

"I can't drink more than one at this time of day—I'll sleep all afternoon!" Foster smiled and she said, "How are the paintings coming along for the next show?"

"Good. I mean, I'm at that stage of wondering whether any of them are good enough, but yeah . . ."

"It's healthy to have doubts, Foster, but you do know you're being modest."

"Some of the time I do. You know, a lot of people say I'm a fraud, that I just got lucky."

He didn't tell her about the letters, because she'd be dismissive, the same way she'd been dismissive of name-calling in the past, and yet she'd still be hurt that someone was saying those things to him.

"We all need some luck to come our way, but you're certainly no fraud, Foster. You know, even when you were tiny, you had all of this in you. It's not even like you were particularly amazing

94

at drawing or painting—there just seemed to be some . . . intimate relationship between you and the paper. I could watch you all day when you were drawing, and what's more, you wouldn't have noticed I was watching. I was always certain you'd end up doing something creative, and when it became art, I wasn't at all surprised. It just fit."

Her words brought back a vivid memory, of being at the big wooden table in his grandparents' kitchen, kneeling on the chair because he was too small to reach otherwise, and leaning over a piece of paper, creating scenes that would have meant nothing to the adults around him but which were fully realized in his own imagination.

And in that memory, Abi was in the kitchen, too, preparing a snack, or hot chocolate in the wintertime. It always seemed to be just the two of them, and to this day he felt she had given more to him than either of his parents. All they had given him was life, and he'd spent most of the last three decades thinking they had been grudging even in the giving of that.

Fifteen

After saying goodbye to Abi, Foster took a table at a coffee shop just along the street and called the number Claudia had sent across to him.

It rang only a couple of times before someone answered, speaking in a South American accent.

"Hello, could I speak with Marianne Tolman, please? My name's Foster Treherne. I think Claudia Meyer called this morning—I'm just following up on that call."

"Please wait."

Too late, he sensed her English wasn't great and that his request had probably been confusing. But a short while later, the receiver was lifted and a brisk but good-humored voice sounded in his ear.

"Claudia! Lovely as it is to hear from you twice in a day, I really do have nothing more to add on the matter we discussed this morning."

"Mrs. Tolman, it's not Claudia. I think I confused your maid. It's Foster Treherne."

Without pause, she said, "Well, *now* I feel foolish. Where are you, Mr. Treherne?"

"I'm sitting outside a coffee shop in Tribeca."

"Then I'll expect you within the hour."

"Thanks, I—"

He stopped when he realized she'd ended the call. He checked his watch. It wouldn't take more than half an hour to get to the Upper East Side, but he finished his coffee in a single gulp and headed off along the street.

Once he was in a cab, he thought back to the brief conversation. She hadn't sounded unfriendly, just businesslike to the point of being abrupt, no words wasted. Josefin Widegren had described her as being "old money," and had speculated about her being married to someone equally "blue-blooded," and that matched his take on the person he'd just spoken to.

As soon as he stepped out of the cab, the liveried doorman greeted him, saying, "Good afternoon, Mr. Treherne. Mrs. Tolman's expecting you."

"Thanks."

It convinced him that just turning up here unannounced wouldn't have worked. And likewise, when he got to her apartment, the door opened on his approach and a maid appeared.

"Good afternoon, Mr. Treherne. Please come in."

"Thank you." She appeared South American, too, but it wasn't the same person he'd spoken to on the phone.

"Would you follow me, please?"

He did, but not before he took a quick look around the spacious entrance hall. There was a Gerhard Richter, a Peter Doig, a Basquiat. She showed him into an equally grand reception room, and now there was almost too much art to absorb—Georg Baselitz, another Doig, Yayoi Kusama, Helen Frankenthaler, Alex Katz, Paula Rego . . .

"Would you like coffee, or something else?"

"No, I'm good, thanks."

"Of course. Please, make yourself comfortable. Mrs. Tolman will be with you shortly."

She left, and Foster took in the room and its collection. He was rich—richer than most people could imagine—and yet there was no way he could afford an apartment like this, let alone the art collection inside it.

He moved around looking at the paintings, as if at a private viewing in a leading gallery. He was studying the Frankenthaler when he heard footsteps behind him, and turned to see a woman who at first glance looked no different to the much younger woman in the photograph of the Piranesi Society—smartly dressed as if just back from a formal lunch, slim, her hair in a similar but updated style.

She smiled as she walked forward, as if this were the most normal thing in the world, and said, "Mr. Treherne, how do you do?"

He shook her hand, finding her grip elusive—no sooner had he made contact than her hand was whisked away again and she was showing him to a chair.

Once he was sitting, he said, "Mrs. Tolman—"

"Please, call me Marianne."

"Of course. Then, likewise, call me Foster."

"I expect you're wondering why I tried to put off your visit. I do dislike people springing things on me, don't you? And in truth, I was a little embarrassed—you see, I own two of your paintings, but as it happens, I have neither in the apartment at the moment."

Foster couldn't imagine her being embarrassed about anything, ever.

But he looked around the room dutifully and said, "I understand, but there isn't a thing in this room that I'd replace with one of mine right now."

She nodded, as if accepting a compliment of her taste. "I continue to acquire, but can't bring myself to sell, so I have a little change-around twice a year. Now, what can I do for you, Foster?"

"You'll have heard the news about my father." She nodded again, but appeared disinclined to add anything in response. "I'm just trying to find out a little more about him, and about my mother, and it seems the best way of doing that is to speak to his former friends in the Piranesi Society." There was no reaction at all to the mention of the society, no surprise, no unease. "So I wanted to ask you about him, that's all."

Did he notice the slightest easing of tension in the room as she smiled and started to speak, saying, "Oh, Charlie was a big character. He could be so much fun, always coming up with some crazy scheme or other. I guess you're like him in that respect." She caught Foster's confused expression and said, "I'm talking about The New Painters—that was your idea, wasn't it?"

"Oh, sure, I see what you mean."

That was one of the myths that had become accepted fact in the accounts of The New Painters, that it had been Foster's scheme. In truth, it had been Polly's idea, and she'd been the driving force behind it from the beginning. Foster had simply become the stand-out success, and so it had made a better story to edit out the input of the others.

"Exactly, and that's how Charlie was. I'm not sure if he came up with the idea of forming a society, but he was absolutely the instigator. So much energy."

"Was he popular?"

"That's not a word I would use. We were a tight-knit group, too tight-knit to be worried about crass things like popularity. We all liked him, that's the important thing—he was the very heart and soul of the Piranesi."

"So you couldn't imagine anyone having a grudge against him, wanting to hurt him, that kind of thing?"

"What an extraordinary question." She looked genuinely bemused. "Charlie was a postgraduate history student from a good family. Why on earth would anyone want to hurt him?"

Foster wasn't sure what being from a good family had to do with anything, and based on his memory of his paternal grandparents, he wasn't convinced they'd been that anyway—at least, not by his definition of "good."

But he decided to take a chance with Marianne Tolman. He was pretty sure she'd have heard from Chris Hamblyn and Jo Widegren, despite their claims of no longer being in touch, but she wouldn't know all of what they'd told Foster. So he'd test the water to see how much they'd really liked Charlie.

"I ask only because other people I've spoken to suggested his behavior could be . . . I don't know, I can't remember the exact word they used, but overbearing, maybe?"

He thought she'd make a show of asking who these people were that he'd spoken to, but instead she shook her head as if deep in thought, and said, "No, I wouldn't hold with that, but I can perhaps see what they're getting at. He was exciting to be around, but there *was* a dangerous quality about him, a feeling that he was always on the verge of doing something he shouldn't do. It was part of what made him thrilling, but yes, I can see how some people might have found it unnerving too."

"Did he actually ever do anything he shouldn't have done?"

"No, I didn't mean it like that. It was more about the perception of danger than the real thing. We were all history students, after all, not desperados."

"I see. I asked only because, well, the primary thing I know about him is that his life ended with him doing something that seems pretty reckless to me." Marianne Tolman stared at him with a fixed expression, an icy politeness that wasn't quite unfriendly, but made her seem as if she were sitting a long way from him. Foster felt an almost visceral urge to shake that demeanor out of her, so he added casually, "That is, of course, if his death was really an accident."

It worked, to some extent, in that she kept her composure but looked at him as if he'd just told her one of the paintings on her walls was a fake. "What on earth are you talking about? Of course it was an accident. I can't begin to think why you might suggest otherwise."

"Why are you so confident it *was* an accident? Until two weeks ago no one knew what had happened to him."

She tensed, looking on the verge of springing from her chair, and said, "I suspect I know what you're getting at, Foster, but let me tell you, Giorgio Pichler's a wonderful person and a man of unquestionable integrity." Foster was ready to ask why she was bringing Giorgio into it, but she appeared to preempt him, saying, "You must know that by suggesting it wasn't an accident you're impugning Giorgio's good character. He said your father walked out alone that day, and I for one don't doubt him for a single moment."

"Are you still in touch with Giorgio?"

"No, I'm not." The fight seemed to go out of her immediately. "I don't know what became of him. We never kept in touch."

Foster nodded, because he'd expected as much. They'd all been so close, and had all thought so highly of Giorgio Pichler—certainly, none of them had suggested he'd been possessive or controlling, as Foster's father had in his journal—and yet not one of them had kept in touch or knew anything about what had happened to him. Foster would have to get Sigrid to track him down, because he was increasingly convinced Giorgio was the key to what had happened to his dad.

Marianne offered what looked like a conciliatory smile, albeit a brittle one, and said, "If you don't mind me saying so, Foster, I hadn't expected this line of questioning from you. All this . . . suspicion."

"I guess that's because I'm struggling to work out the dynamic of the Piranesi Society. I have my dad's journal, so there are references to how close you all were, but hints of tensions, too, and then all this business about raiding locked cemeteries and visiting historic monastery libraries. So naturally, I'm wondering if secrets are being kept from me—you have to accept that it all sounds a little mysterious."

"Don't you see? That was the whole point." He noticed her face had softened a little more, suggesting she thought she'd averted a potential trap. "You know how it is when you're young—you want the world to be so much more mysterious than it really is. I was completely swept up in it at the time; I'm sure the others were too. But life moves on, we grow up, we see the world as it really is."

"You mean, you no longer believe in all that lost knowledge waiting to be found?"

To his surprise, she said, "In truth, I'm confident there are still many great secrets to be found in archaeological sites and ancient libraries. We didn't find any, and it's easy to be embarrassed by our youthful exploits thirty years on, but our endeavor was serious, Foster, deadly serious, and given a little more time together, who knows what we might have discovered."

It was the second time one of them had used the phrase "deadly serious," but before he had a chance to ask another question, the door opened and the maid who'd greeted Foster stepped inside. Marianne turned and acknowledged her presence with a slight nod of the head, then turned back to him.

"I'm so sorry, but I was being truthful when I told Claudia I was incredibly busy today. I really do have to go."

She stood, and Foster stood with her and said, "Of course. Well, thanks for seeing me anyway—I appreciate it can't have been easy."

She was relaxed now that the conversation was coming to a close. "It was a delight. I only wish we'd had longer."

She gestured for him to follow her and then walked him to the front door.

As they moved back through the hall, Foster said, "I'm sorry if some of my questions seemed . . . well, you know. It's been a pretty crazy couple of weeks for me. I'm still trying to get my head around most of it."

"I'm sure you are, and there's no need at all to apologize." The maid had opened the front door for him, and now Marianne turned and shook his hand, then smiled. "You know, Ham said you were just like Charlie, and I can see what he meant, because you do look like him, but having met you, I think you're very much your own man. Yes, absolutely your own man."

"Thanks." She was still smiling, the warmest he'd seen her look during the entire visit.

But as he made his way down in the elevator, past the doorman and out of the building—"Good day to you, Mr. Treherne"—he turned over her final comment again and again. It had clearly been intended as a compliment, but her words begged a couple of questions.

When had she heard from Chris Hamblyn, who'd claimed he couldn't even remember her name and knew nothing about what had become of her? And given Charlie had been such a close friend and so exciting to be around—the very heart and soul of the Piranesi—why would Marianne be as pleased as she'd appeared to be to discover that Foster was so unlike him?

Sixteen

Return flights from the US always gave him jetlag, even from New York, the unusual result of which was that for a few days after arriving back he was awake at a time most people would have considered normal. So it was just after nine when he strolled into the office the next morning, early enough that Natsuko and Maja weren't even there yet.

Axel said, "Morning, Foster, how was your trip?"

"It was okay." Axel poured him a coffee and handed it to him. "Thanks."

"And the funeral?"

"Yeah. It's weird having a funeral for someone you didn't know. Though I feel like I'm getting to know him now somehow."

Axel laughed. "My father's still alive and I probably know him less than you do yours."

"I'm sure that isn't true." But Foster laughed, too.

Then Axel's expression changed, like he was ready to break bad news, and he said, "Sigrid's here." Foster looked around, but Axel added, "I put her in the studio. I think she's sleeping now."

Sigrid was a great private detective, but she had one particular weakness that she jokingly called her "professional cliché."

"Has she been drinking again?"

"I think so. She was waiting in the doorway when I arrived, said she had some important information for you. But when she stood up, she appeared . . . not very able. I put a drop cloth on the couch, and told her to wait there. I checked on her about fifteen minutes ago. Sleeping."

"Okay, I guess I'll leave her a while longer."

He noticed the mail had arrived and that Axel had placed it on Natsuko's desk. As Axel went back to his own desk, Foster sifted idly through the letters and pulled out the one he'd expected to find there, with the address in Comic Sans. He opened it and read the note inside.

Eight months until your moment of truth. When the world learns what you know already. You're a fraud.

Foster hadn't seen all the notes that had arrived in the last few weeks, but of all those he'd seen over the last year or so, none had previously had a date-specific comment like this. The author was clearly referring to his next show. He knew how Natsuko would react, telling him that this elevated the threat to a possible security risk, and maybe Werner and Claudia would think the same—Werner most of all, given that the letters had all been mailed from within Europe.

The street door opened and Natsuko came in. After all the initial greetings were out of the way, she looked down at the open note on her desk, then picked it up and studied it for longer than seemed necessary for so few words.

When she spoke, her voice was grave. "This has to go across to Sigrid."

"Thought you'd say that. I'll take it to her now." Natsuko looked puzzled and Foster smiled and said, "She was here when Axel arrived, so he put her on the couch in the studio."

"Ah," said Natsuko, needing no additional explanation.

Foster slipped the note into his pocket, poured an extra cup of coffee, and walked through to the studio. Sigrid was still sleeping, snoring gently, a youthful quality about her in that unguarded moment.

He wasn't sure how old she was, though he guessed around sixty. With her high cheekbones, piercing blue eyes, and slightly wild gray hair, she looked too distinctive to be a private investigator, and could easily pass for an artist herself. With the suit and the brogues, she might also pass for a former member of the Piranesi Society.

With that thought, he glanced down at the leather satchel-style briefcase, wondering if the news she'd come to share was about his father's former friends.

"Is that coffee for me?"

It was as if she had never truly been asleep, and that a natural defense mechanism had alerted her partly conscious brain to the fact that someone had an eye on her briefcase.

He looked at her and smiled, and said, "It is. Heavy night?"

"Could say that." She sat up and reached out for the coffee. She took a gulp and nodded, as if to suggest that was enough for a full recovery. "Okay, sit down, I have things to tell you."

The chairs and coffee table that Axel had set out for Daniela Herrera's last visit were still there, so Foster moved one over to face Sigrid. At the same time, she reached down for her briefcase and took out some papers. She handed one to him, a list of towns and cities.

"Where the postmarks are legible, all of these towns have sent the Comic Sans letters. As you can see, they come from all over Europe." She handed him a second sheet, once again with a list of place names. "However, sixty percent are from within a limited geographical area. You see, France, Belgium, Luxembourg, Germany, and the Netherlands are all represented here, but none of the towns is particularly far from the others." She handed him another sheet of paper, this one with a map on which all the various towns and cities from which letters had been sent to him had a black dot over them. In the center of the map, a single town had a blue dot. "You see here how the dots are concentrated in a small field, but right in the center of that field is Maastricht. Remember, you've been receiving these letters since two years now, and not one came from Maastricht. I thought that was unusual."

He looked at the map again, at the blue dot over the Dutch city. He understood Sigrid's logic, and also the logic of the perpetrator. Of course, if they'd been really smart, they'd have sent the letters from their hometown and used Maastricht as a decoy.

"So you think the person behind this is there?"

Sigrid held her finger up, telling him to be patient, though that allowed Foster to see that her hand was trembling.

"I decided to do some searching, to find out if anyone you dealt with in the past might now be living in Maastricht, and guess what, I got a result. Your ex-girlfriend."

His first thought was of Nele, but he realized that was too recent. There weren't too many before her, but he went through them, discounting each in turn for one reason or another, almost feeling he didn't want to reach the ultimate destination his memory was tumbling toward.

Rather than say her name himself, he said, "Which ex-girlfriend?"

"Polly Carmichael. It makes sense if you think about it. You were together when you both set up The New Painters, but you became famous and she didn't, and then you broke up."

"Polly lives in Maastricht?"

"Yes. She's married, has a little girl, two years old. She's still an artist, makes some money from it, but not a great deal. I don't think they're poor, but . . . not rich."

"Polly never cared about money."

"Did she care about success?"

You must come to my flat, Polly had said when they'd first met, only weeks into their first term. She'd shared an apartment in an old building with a boy and a girl from their course—Ben and Kami, who'd both become part of The New Painters and whose work was hanging on the walls of Foster's loft, though he didn't know what either of them was doing now.

There had been an instant chemistry between Foster and Polly, but that first invite had been about something else—it had been the excitement of enlisting a kindred spirit. Polly had been a connector from the start, and her apartment, with its high-ceilinged rooms that never seemed to get warm in winter, became the central hub for their group of friends, the place where they would always end their evenings, more often than not discussing the art world rather than art itself.

It had been her idea, too—The New Painters—and she'd dreamed so much of how successful they would *all* be, but particularly the two of them, Foster and Polly. For so long it had been her circus, and then within weeks it had been snatched away from her and handed to Foster. And he knew how much that must have hurt, yet still he could not believe what Sigrid was telling him.

Foster held up the pieces of paper and said, "This is impressive, Sigrid, but I think you've got the wrong person. Polly has every reason to be resentful, but she wouldn't do this kind of thing."

"Are you confident you knew her so well? And what about her husband, Kurt? I think you didn't know him at all, no? Maybe Kurt defends the honor of his wife. I see you disagree, but I've observed similar situations many times, and soon enough we find out who's right."

"What do you mean?"

As if it should have been obvious, she said, "I've had a watch put on them, just to be in no doubt."

He felt his stomach sinking. He couldn't believe Polly was behind these letters, but even if she were, he didn't see how spying on her was a justifiable response. It made him feel cheap, and sordid in some way. Added to that, if word got out it would be a PR disaster.

"I appreciate your thinking, Sigrid, and I know you're doing all this to protect me, but I don't want Polly under surveillance on my account. I want you to get it stopped."

She looked puzzled, trying to figure out what his objection could be, and said, "It won't need to be for very long. If we can get proof, then very quickly we can get a legal letter sent to them, and if necessary, an injunction. But in my experience, when the person concerned knows that their identity has been discovered, they cease."

"I don't care. I want it stopped. I don't believe it's her anyway, but even if you're right, you'll have to find out some other way. I won't allow this."

"As you wish." Her disagreement was clear from her curt tone, but she added, "I'll see to it as soon as I return to the office."

"Thank you."

He thought of the letter in his pocket, but decided against giving it to Sigrid now. Like Natsuko, she'd see an implied threat in the reference to his next show, and she'd use that to argue the case again for keeping Polly under surveillance.

Instead, he changed the subject, saying, "I thought you'd called round because you'd found out something about the photograph." She raised her eyebrows, as if to ask him which photograph he was talking about. "My parents and their friends at Bologna."

"Ah, that! No, it's very difficult to establish identities of people from an old picture like that. But there is something very interesting about your photograph." She reached out and took the sheets of paper from him, then put them in the briefcase and searched for the envelope containing her copy of the photograph. She took it out and handed him the picture. "There's something strange. Can you see what it is?"

He felt his blood spike slightly, thinking back to that expression on Chris Hamblyn's face, the thing he'd seen that had alarmed him. But the feeling ebbed when he looked at the photograph, because it looked the same to Foster as it had every time previously.

"I don't know. The only thing I think each time I look at it is that it . . . it's badly posed. The composition is wrong."

She pointed at him with a smile. "Yes! Yes, Foster, exactly, and it doesn't take an artist to notice. I noticed it too. The composition is wrong, because somebody has been airbrushed from this picture. The man in the white shirt and the cravat . . ."

"Giorgio Pichler."

"Whatever. Someone was standing behind him. If you look on his right shoulder, the white of the shirt is smudged somehow? I think the person behind had his hand on his friend Giorgio's shoulder there."

Now that Foster looked, he could see it—not so much the blurring of the white where Sigrid imagined a hand had been airbrushed out, but the space behind Giorgio and next to Marianne. If somebody were standing there, it would bring the composition together again, and in many ways, that missing person would then become almost the central focus of the photograph.

But Sigrid hadn't finished yet.

"Now, prepare to be amazed. It's not surprising that you didn't see this. But I'm warning you now, once you do see it, you will see it every time. On the step, between this Giorgio's leg and the foot of the lady to the right, the person who airbrushed the photograph missed the toecap of a shoe."

He held the photograph closer, but the action became redundant almost immediately. Now that Sigrid had mentioned it, Foster could clearly see the edge of a shoe. He might have looked at it a thousand times, but now he couldn't help but see it. Someone had been standing there, and a part of that person's shoe was still visible in the picture—a man's shoe, he guessed, even from this indistinct evidence.

That was what Chris Hamblyn had noticed: a crucial piece of evidence in that photograph, something they'd meant to erase. The Piranesi Society had consisted of seven members, not six, and among the many small lies they'd told, Chris Hamblyn and Josefin Widegren had both failed to mention this seventh person, or to admit that the photograph had been doctored to make that person disappear.

Seventeen

Foster handed the photograph back to Sigrid and said, "I think I might be able to solve this. I'm pretty certain I have a copy of the original in storage in New York."

"Then it's unfortunate I didn't speak with you before you went."

"No problem. I'll get Benny to FedEx it across."

Sigrid stood, looking momentarily unsteady but getting her balance, and said, "Not that it will help me much. As I said to you before, identifying people from a past photo isn't easy, unless you have access to one or more of their friends from that time."

Foster nodded. He had access of a sort to some of them, but he couldn't imagine they'd be in any hurry to identify the missing person or the reason for his being airbrushed from the picture.

"So, I'll leave you now, but I'll be in touch. Please, don't get up."

Foster had been midway to standing himself, but fell back again readily, hit by a wave of fatigue.

"Thanks, Sigrid. See you soon."

"Naturally."

She walked out and Foster leaned back in his chair. He didn't have the energy to go back up to the apartment and get his father's notebook, so he was reduced to trying to recall what he'd seen written there. Crucially, he couldn't remember another initial. If the missing person from the photograph had been a member of the

Piranesi Society, surely his dad would have referred to him once or twice in his journal?

This development also changed another dynamic. Foster had felt they'd all been trying to protect Giorgio Pichler, claiming not to know what had become of him, maybe because they'd known there'd been some tension between Giorgio and Charlie, and because it was a matter of public record that Giorgio had been the only person on that trip with Charlie.

But that was as nothing compared with the level of deception surrounding the identity and whereabouts of this seventh person. A photograph had been airbrushed, and none of the three members of the society who Foster had spoken to had mentioned anything about the person who'd been hidden. Even if they'd left the Piranesi behind thirty years ago, it seemed they were still closing ranks to protect one of their own.

Foster was distracted from his thoughts by a screech of brakes somewhere out in the street. There was no other noise afterward, but Foster held his breath, listening. Silence followed, and he started to breathe again, but a short while later, Maja came bursting into the studio.

"Foster, you should come. Quickly. Sigrid's been killed!"

The fatigue evaporated. He flew from the seat and had caught up with Maja even before she reached the office, and he overtook her then, running out of the building. Axel and Natsuko and three other people—including the badly shaken driver—were gathered around Sigrid, who lay in the street. Her briefcase had landed fifteen feet away.

Axel and a passerby were tending to Sigrid.

The driver, who was German but speaking in English to Natsuko, kept repeating, "There was nothing I could do. She just stumbled. I couldn't do anything. I braked. But she stumbled right into the car."

Natsuko was resting a comforting hand on the man's arm, but then Axel looked up and said, "It's okay, she's breathing. I think she broke a leg, and maybe got a concussion, but . . ."

Foster felt an urge to go and pick up the briefcase, not because he needed anything that was in it, or even because Sigrid would need it, but because there was something terrible about seeing it abandoned there like that.

First, he said, "Has anyone called for an ambulance?"

The woman who was next to Axel looked up and said, "Yes, I just called already."

"So did we," said the other woman who was standing nearby, and Foster realized now that she was with the man in the car.

"Good. Should we try to move her?"

"No!" It was the woman who was with Axel, her voice urgent. "It's important to keep her like this until the ambulance arrives. If there's damage we can make it worse by moving her."

Foster nodded, and his mind involuntarily skipped back to the strange topography of his father's corpse beneath that sheet at the forensic institute, to the damage that had been done to his body in the fall, then in the thirty-two years of gradually being ground and twisted as the glacier pushed ever down the valley.

Sigrid moaned, a relief in itself, and Axel said, "It's okay, Sigrid, you've been in an accident, but an ambulance is coming."

She uttered a couple of expletives in German, which in turn set the driver off defending himself again, and Natsuko calming and reassuring him. Foster looked down at Sigrid—her eyes were open now, and apart from the strange angle of her left leg, she looked remarkably well.

She saw him and tried a smile as she said, "This was most unprofessional."

"It would certainly be an inconvenience if you got yourself killed. Good investigators are hard to find."

She closed her eyes briefly and said, "Don't worry, an ambulance is coming." She spoke as if she'd called it herself.

The woman who was helping to tend to her looked up at Foster now and said, "Are you the artist Foster Treherne?"

She was in her twenties, pretty, something about her that made him think she might be a student.

"Yes, I am."

"Wow, I love your work."

"Thank you. This is my studio, right here."

She glanced past him, then said, "I think I kind of knew it was around here somewhere, but I never would've known this was it."

He nodded and for a moment became suspicious—of what she might have been doing out here on the street, wondering if she might be the kind of person to send Comic Sans notes. Then he remembered what Sigrid had told him, that the writer of those notes was most likely in Maastricht, most likely someone he'd let down in the past. And this young woman in front of him was exactly what she seemed, an innocent witness to an accident who just happened to like his art.

He looked across the street and said, "I better just get Sigrid's briefcase."

"My briefcase," said Sigrid urgently.

"I'm getting it. Stay calm."

He walked over and picked up the case, and he could hear an ambulance now and was grateful—without being sure why—that he would be spared any additional conversation with the woman tending to Sigrid. Maybe it was just that his mind was too wrapped up in the mysteries of affairs that were over three decades in the past to be engaging in affairs of his own right now.

Foster handed the briefcase to Axel as the ambulance turned into the bottom of the street, followed by a police car.

Immediately, Natsuko said, "We'll take care of this now, Foster. No reason for you to be involved."

Axel nodded, saying, "I'll go to the hospital with her."

"Okay. Sigrid, I'll come see you as soon as you're settled."

"You don't have to."

"But I will."

She laughed once, finding it a struggle.

Foster offered a polite smile to the young woman, then turned and headed back into the studio. Maja was standing behind her desk, ashen-faced.

"Relax, Maja, she's alive." She put a hand to her chest and sighed heavily. "Broken leg, maybe some other injuries, but hopefully she'll be okay."

"I was so afraid!"

"I know, but it's okay." He looked around the office, the jetlag confusion sinking back in, then said, "I think I'm gonna paint for a while."

"Sure. Is there anything you need me to do?"

He was about to tell her to relax, have a coffee, let the shock subside, but he could see she *needed* something to do, something beyond her regular work.

"Actually, yeah, could you email Benny for me? Mark it 'Urgent.'" She grabbed a pen and a notepad and started writing. "Tell him to take a look in the small storeroom. There are some boxes on one of the shelves at the back. One of them has *Charles Treherne* written on the front of it. I want him to FedEx that one to me, fast as possible."

She looked up. "That it?"

"Yeah."

"I'll get right on it."

"Thanks, Maja."

And he walked on. He wanted to look in his dad's journal again, to look for the clues to the identity of that seventh person, but that could wait. It was too long since he'd painted, and the need for it was beginning to eat away at him. He would paint, and then he'd be able to sleep again, and *then* he'd find out how his father had died.

Eighteen

Foster was once again immersed in the new painting, but this time there was no doubt in his mind—this was a glacial landscape he was working on. He was feeling his way into it and across the canvas, feeling the hidden crevasses, feeling the cold, the isolation.

He continued to work the landscape, always aware of what he was not painting—the small, lonely figure at its center. He'd fought against the idea for a while, thinking it clichéd to respond to the discovery of his father's body by painting something so obviously representative. Worse than clichéd, was it exploitative, a brazen play for sympathy?

He thought of the Comic Sans writer—still picturing some anonymous failed artist rather than Polly or even her husband—and how they'd predicted in one of the notes that he would use and exploit the discovery of his father's body. It was an easy accusation to make, an impossible one to refute.

And yet he had to paint it, even knowing full well that the critics would laud it and the naysayers would join together in a Comic Sans chorus. So there would be a figure, in time, but for now he wanted only to paint the landscape itself, the ice.

He'd been working on and off for the last twenty-four hours. He hadn't been to see Sigrid yet, despite wanting to find the time. He hadn't eaten or slept properly. He hadn't thought any more about his father's journal or the person missing from the photograph of the Piranesi Society. He'd only painted.

It was just after eleven in the morning when the studio door opened and Werner, Foster's Berlin gallerist, came in. Foster stopped what he was doing, stepped back, then turned to face him.

Whereas Claudia was a no-nonsense powerhouse, the kind of person who could clear her throat and reduce a room to silence, Werner had the demeanor of an academic specializing in an obscure subject. He always wore a tweed jacket and tortoiseshell glasses. But it was a deceptive look, lulling people into underestimating him, because when it came to business, Werner was just as tough as Claudia.

"Morning, Werner."

Werner acknowledged the greeting, but said, "Why are you painting at this time of day?"

"Came back from New York, day before yesterday."

"Of course." He pointed at the glacial wastes of the canvas Foster was working on. "I *like* that. I like it very much. How many figures are you thinking of?"

"Originally, three, almost filling the canvas. Now I can think only of one small figure, lost right in the middle of it. And I know that might be seen as a predictable response, so it's possible this one'll get nixed before the show."

Werner shook his head. "Since when did you care what other people think? Your instincts are always good, so if you want to paint a solo figure, you do that." He turned to look at some of the other canvases. "Are all of these finished? They all look finished to me."

Foster pointed and said, "Those three on that wall, I guess I'm done with. These over here . . ." Even as he looked at them he could feel a nagging in his mind, a sense that each of those paintings still needed something else, some reworking, some addition. "I'm not sure. We'll have to see about those."

"Good. I think this all looks great. I was talking with Claudia last evening. We both think this could be your best show yet. There's already a lot of buzz, and we still have eight months to go."

"We'll see. You want coffee?"

"No, thank you. I was just in the neighborhood—I'm having lunch with a collector." He gestured toward the canvas. "Keep painting!"

Then he turned and made his way out, and Foster did keep painting. He worked on and off through the afternoon and into early evening, then showered and went to visit Sigrid in the hospital.

She was sitting up on the bed wearing a Chinese-style brocade dressing gown. Her leg was in plaster, but otherwise she looked well. She was watching a detective show on the TV, but turned it off as soon as she saw him.

"Foster! How good of you. And I must buy a gift for your Axel—he was such an angel."

"He'd like that." He put the chocolates and flowers he'd brought on the nightstand next to the bed. "How are you feeling?"

"Like a fool. But let that be a lesson to me."

"Will it?"

"Maybe." She pointed to a brown envelope that was on the chair near the bed. "Pass me that and sit down. My assistant came."

He did as she told him, but said, "You have an assistant?"

"How could you not know this? You think I'm some kind of one-person operation?" The chastisement was laced with humor, but he had genuinely thought she *was* a one-woman outfit. "So, I didn't cancel the surveillance on your ex-girlfriend, because, well, you know the story."

Foster felt his blood spike. And he knew why. He'd wanted Sigrid to stop the surveillance not just because of how tawdry it seemed, but because at some level he feared she'd be proved right.

"It might have been too late anyway, because my Dutch contact worked quickly. We have some clear results already."

"I'm not sure I want to know what they are."

"Oh, but you do. It isn't your ex-girlfriend sending the letters, or not directly."

She handed him the envelope and he pulled out a series of photographs. There were five in total, each showing a man in a suit, each showing him dropping a letter in a mailbox in a different location. Foster was horrified, seeing immediately that Sigrid's Dutch contact had tailed this guy daily.

"How long has this operation been live?"

"Just over a week. I thought you might try to put a stop to it, so I decided to instigate first, let you know later."

"And you've had someone tailing him?"

Sigrid smiled. "You make it sound so melodramatic. It really isn't. But yes, someone followed him just enough to witness this. He's a sales representative for a software company."

"And who is he?"

"Polly Carmichael's husband, Kurt. So yes, it's possible he mails the letters on her behalf, but also that he does it without her knowledge. I did mention that possibility. But I guess now we'll never know."

She was goading him into giving the okay for the surveillance to continue, but he wouldn't allow it, and was uncomfortable even with this level of intrusion.

Foster said, "Have you told your Dutch contact to call off the surveillance?"

"I've told them to put a temporary stop on it, but that was only this afternoon, so it's easy to begin again if you want certainty."

He flicked through the pictures again. Despite himself, he was sorry Polly didn't appear in any of them—he was curious to see how she looked now, ten years on.

"No, I don't want it to start again and I don't want certainty. I had you look into these letters in case there was a threat—"

"There still could be a threat."

Foster held out the photographs and said, "Look at him, Sigrid. This guy isn't about to turn up at my opening and attack me. He's just a guy who's angry because his wife never got the fame she deserved, so he's venting at the ex-boyfriend who got all the gifts. He's no threat."

"Trust me, Foster, ordinary people do terrible things."

"Not this ordinary person," he said, looking at the top photograph again. Kurt looked too ordinary for Polly, too safe and middle-of-the-road. But maybe after Foster, middle-of-the-road and baggage-free was what she'd wanted, and he could hardly blame her for that.

THE DAILY TELEGRAPH— JUNE 19TH 2010

The New Painters have no manifesto as such, but many of the group are eloquent and forthright in explaining their vision, and in large part, the obvious quality of their work justifies this youthful swagger.

Yet ironically, it's the least eloquent of the dozen—the young American artist Foster Treherne—who has been the standout success of the show. When pressed on the message he's trying to convey in his luminous figurative paintings, Treherne said, "I don't know what I'm trying to say. I only know that I need to paint." And the rest, as they say, is silence.

Nineteen

By the next day his sleep pattern had returned to normal, and it was just before lunch when he got down to the office. He immediately saw that the FedEx package had arrived, and as soon as he'd said his good mornings to the team, he walked over to it.

Natsuko said, "Another letter, too."

She held up a Comic Sans note, though he was too far away to see what it said. He felt a wave of discomfort with the thought that Polly's husband had probably been photographed sending it, the last action of Sigrid's Dutch contact before she'd called off the surveillance.

"You can file it, but I don't think we need to worry about them so much anymore. Sigrid found out who it is."

All three of them looked shocked and expectant.

Foster shrugged. "It's either my ex-girlfriend's husband or both of them working together. She's an artist, so they're just bitter, not dangerous."

Natsuko said, "Oh my goodness, Foster. This is the girlfriend who was in The New Painters with you?"

"Yeah, the same one. And she was good, and she's still working as an artist . . ." He thought of the day ahead then, and said to Maja, "Are Rolf and Tim coming by today?"

She glanced at her diary. "Yes, this afternoon."

"Good. Tell them the three paintings on the left-hand wall are ready to go into storage. They're done."

"I'll do that."

"Thanks. Any more news on Sigrid this morning?"

Axel said, "They're hoping she'll be released this afternoon. She's going to spend some time recovering with her mother."

"Her mother's still alive?"

Axel laughed, but looked embarrassed that he was laughing at Sigrid's expense. "We were shocked, too. Apparently she's ninety-one, but still healthy."

"Okay." Foster picked up the box. "I'm taking this upstairs, but I'm around if anyone needs me."

He left them and went back to his apartment and put the box on the dining table. As he opened it, he couldn't recall looking through it in the past, and yet he must have done so because he definitely remembered seeing that photograph before.

He emptied the contents out across the table before dropping the empty box onto the floor. There were a lot of photographs, many of them the kind of cheap snapshots of the period, and some of those had bleached so that the pictures were no longer so clear. There were postcards, and plenty of tickets and paper guides to various museums, too—all of them from Europe—as well as a few leaflets or circulars from the history department at Bologna.

Foster picked up a snapshot of four guys standing with their arms around each other. One of them was clearly his father, looking even younger than in the Piranesi photograph, but he didn't recognize the others. Maybe it had been taken at Yale, or even in high school, and he wondered how it had ended up in this box and not one of the others. Then he turned it over and noticed a smudged trace of blue putty in each of the four corners.

And now he understood what this box contained. It was the contents of his dad's dorm room in Bologna, the pictures he'd stuck to the wall, the various mementoes he'd kept from his travels, paperwork relating to his studies. Someone had been given the task of emptying that room after Charlie's disappearance, and boxing up its contents for his parents.

He'd never had much, if any, love for his Treherne grandparents. He'd preferred them to the Fosters, though that hadn't amounted to much of a competition. Now though, he felt badly for them, thinking of them receiving this pathetic box of possessions, slowly coming to terms with the fact that it was the only part of their son that would ever return to them.

Except, of course, something else of Charlie *had* returned to them, his own son, and they had rejected that grandson for too long, and even later had done only the bare minimum to acknowledge him. Yet standing here over these scattered memories, Foster thought he understood something of their pain and wished he had taken the time to speak with them before their own deaths.

He sifted through another pile and there he saw the photograph he'd been looking for. It was on better-quality paper than the snapshots, and had not faded. He picked it up and smiled with satisfaction at the sight of the young man with brown hair in a neat side-parting, wearing what looked like a red velvet jacket over a white shirt, standing in exactly the position Sigrid had suggested, his hand resting on Giorgio's shoulder just as she'd said it would.

Foster pulled a chair free from the table and sat, staring at the face of the young man who'd been airbrushed out. He had a wry smile, one eyebrow raised, a look of entitlement and privilege about him, although, given the playful poses being struck by Charlie and Lucy, Foster couldn't be sure if that was just an act for the camera.

"Who are you?" Foster whispered, and in his thoughts he asked the additional question, *And why were you airbrushed from this picture?* It wasn't just the matter of why he'd been removed, but why the other members of the Piranesi Society had agreed to it and been willing to lie—albeit a lie of omission—on their friend's behalf. What had he done that his identity needed to be concealed now?

Foster got up again and placed the picture at one end of the table, then started to sort everything else. The various leaflets, tickets, and other ephemera went into the middle of the table, along with letters and postcards. Photographs that weren't from Bologna went at the other end, whereas those that featured any member of the Piranesi Society or looked as if they might have been taken in Italy were placed around the group portrait.

There was a picture of his mom and dad sitting at a table outside a café, both wearing sunglasses, laughing spontaneously, too happily in the moment even to be aware that the photograph was being taken. There was a picture of Charlie and Giorgio in hiking gear somewhere in the mountains. Several showed various members of the group in ornate libraries or walking about ancient graveyards. Then there was a picture of everyone except Giorgio—who'd possibly been wielding the camera—standing next to a misty lake, all wearing long coats and scarves, like a fashion shoot portraying a romanticized version of youthful academia.

The more he looked, the more he felt the now-familiar envy creeping back in. The photographs were probably no more representative of their everyday reality than Foster's Instagram page was of his own daily life, but still they suggested a sense of adventure and romance and a closeness that he could not recall from his own youth. Even the camaraderie of The New Painters had been something of an act, draped over the naked ambition that had really driven them.

But Foster was struck by something else, too, and he wasn't sure if it tempered his envy or intensified it. There wasn't a single photograph among the Italian shots that featured anyone beyond the seven in that group shot of the Piranesi Society. That's how close they'd been, that their entire social world had been encapsulated in that group of seven, but maybe that in itself explained his father's growing sense of unease, that things had become too incestuous, that the closeness had transformed into something malignant.

What else would explain the secrecy exhibited by the three survivors he'd spoken to so far? They'd lied about keeping in touch with each other, they'd concealed the existence of a seventh member of the group, and they had surely lied about the circumstances surrounding Charlie Treherne's death.

Foster picked up another picture showing that anonymous seventh member, sitting in an ornate wooden chair, posing, his chin raised, his face looking off to one side, like a Romantic hero. In the foreground was the back of someone's head, a shoulder, and the sketch pad on which she was drawing the sitter's portrait. Chris Hamblyn had told Foster that his mother had been a talented artist, but even without that intelligence he would have known that it was Lucy. What he really needed to know was the identity of the man she was drawing.

Sigrid was out of commission for the foreseeable future, but Foster remembered Daniela Herrera's offer of help, and felt a telltale eagerness to latch on to that offer. She'd just been doing her job in looking after Foster, but still he wanted to see her. He called down to Natsuko and asked for her number, then dialed.

It went to voicemail and he said, "Daniela, this is Foster Treherne. You did say I should call if I needed anything, and my private investigator has been in an accident, so . . . I was hoping you might be able to help me identify a man who my father knew. It could be important. Er . . . Yeah, give me a call, or drop by if you like—if you can help, that is. Thanks."

As he hung up he realized he'd sounded like a complete space cadet. He should have had Natsuko make the call for him.

Twenty

The next day he had a photoshoot for an interview in a Japanese art magazine that he'd done weeks ago. The photographer had flown out from Japan with a crew of four. They spent an hour in the apartment, then wanted some shots in the studio with paintings in the background, but because Foster didn't want any of the new work in the piece, they had to call Rolf and Tim to collect some of his older paintings from storage. While they waited, the photographer took Foster outside for some "street-style guerilla" shots.

They were back in the studio when the door opened and Daniela stepped inside. She waved briefly but then retreated into the office. He'd noticed she was wearing jeans and a casual top rather than the work clothes he'd seen her in previously. He was pleased to see her—more than pleased—and he liked the way she looked in civilian clothes.

The photographer was finished within ten minutes or so, but it took another thirty to get him and his crew out of the building, as all five of them gave Foster small gifts and thanked him and engaged in what seemed like an endless farewell. His heart sank as they made a hesitant progression through the office, because Daniela Herrera was no longer there.

Once they'd gone, he said to Natsuko, "Where's Daniela?"

"She just popped out to make a phone call. Said she'd be back in a minute." He hadn't seen her out in the street as he'd waved off the Japanese delegation, and wondered if the phone call had been a ruse, or she'd had a change of heart about helping him. As if reading his thoughts, Natsuko said, "She'll be back."

"Good. I'm just going upstairs to get something. If she comes back, *don't* let her leave."

He went up to the apartment and picked up the group photograph of the Piranesi Society. By the time he got back into the office, Daniela was sitting on the edge of Natsuko's desk, but she stood now.

"Sorry about that. I had to take a call. I walked around the block but it's a bigger block than I thought."

Axel was making fresh coffee and called over, "Coffee, Foster?"

"Please." Foster turned back to Daniela and led the way over to the reception area as he said, "I appreciate you coming. And you're not wearing office clothes."

"No, I'm not." They sat as she continued, saying, "The US government does believe in aiding American citizens wherever it can, and I did offer to help if I could, but stepping into the role of your incapacitated PI isn't strictly what I'd had in mind, or indeed, within my remit."

"I guess when you put it like that." Clearly, he'd been too successful and too spoiled for too long. "So . . . ?"

She shrugged. "I have a ton of annual leave I haven't used, and I'm a fan, and I'm interested in helping if I can. Within limits, of course."

Axel brought two mugs of coffee over and put them on the table between them, making a show of not wanting to interrupt.

They thanked him anyway, and Foster said, "That means a lot to me, Daniela, I'm grateful."

He placed the picture on the table and she reached over and picked it up.

"What's this?"

"The picture they used in the *Times*. Sigrid noticed someone had been airbrushed out of it and I remembered I had an original copy. The guy in the red jacket. I need to find out who he is, why he was removed, why the others were all happy to lie about it."

She was nodding as he spoke, but she stared intently at the photograph the whole time. And she continued to stare once he'd finished, a frown across her brow, a look of intense concentration.

Finally, she put the picture on her lap and started searching for something on her phone, and after a minute of that, she smiled and said, "I knew it." She passed both the phone and the photograph back to Foster. "Thirty years on, he doesn't even look much older, but it's him, I'd swear on it."

Foster looked down at the picture on her phone. As she'd suggested, it was a man who didn't even look dramatically older, his hair still in the same style and still suspiciously the same color. It was him, and Foster was as impressed at the speed with which she'd identified him as if she'd performed a magic trick.

"Who is this?"

"That's Gregory Tolman."

"The fintech guy?"

"The fintech guy."

He handed the phone back to her, but pointed at the photograph now, the pieces falling together even as he spoke.

"This person is Marianne Arthur. Chris Hamblyn claimed he couldn't remember her second name, presumably because he didn't want me to track her down. I met her last week in New York. She's now Marianne Tolman—she was Gregory Tolman's first wife." Now he pointed at Tolman himself. "He was airbrushed from the picture, and none of them wanted me to find out about him. Why?"

Daniela raised her eyebrows, sounding intrigued as she said, "I have no idea, but I'd be curious to find out."

"Me too, which brings us to the more important question—how do I get in touch with this guy?"

Daniela laughed a little. "Um, you don't? Billionaire, rumored to be making a run for New York mayor next time around. His number isn't in the book, probably not even in the books you have access to, and if he went to this much trouble, he's not gonna want to speak with you."

Foster nodded, accepting her point, but then something else occurred to him.

"I'll be back in a minute."

He went up to the loft and got his dad's notebook, and as soon as he was sitting back with Daniela he skipped through it looking at the initials. And only now did he see it, that there were two almost identical references, "G" and "Gi", but until now Foster had missed the "i" in the second, mistaking it in his father's dense script for some sort of punctuation—a comma or semicolon.

Gi was Giorgio. But G was the person who'd been too controlling, who'd become borderline creepy, who'd filled Charlie with misgivings. And now Foster knew that the person who'd been the subject of all those troubled comments was not Giorgio Pichler, but Gregory Tolman.

They'd all pleaded ignorance of the whereabouts of Giorgio Pichler, arousing Foster's suspicions, and maybe Giorgio did have something to hide—after all, he'd been the only one there with Charlie on that trip. But their secrecy surrounding Giorgio might equally have been nothing more than a distraction, pulling Foster's attention away from the person who'd been airbrushed from that photograph.

Twenty-One

He put the notebook on the table and walked across to the main part of the office. Axel and Maja were looking at him, waiting for instructions.

"I need you to find out everything you can about Gregory Tolman, the fintech billionaire. Start with Wikipedia and take it from there. And there's a company in New York that Claudia used once before, specializing in corporate intelligence or something like that."

Maja said, "I remember, the guy who used to work for Kroll. I may even have the contact on file. If not, I'll ask Claudia."

"Good." Foster turned to Natsuko. "Could you . . . No, maybe better if I do it myself."

He took his phone and called Chris Hamblyn's number without even being sure what he was about to say. In the end it didn't matter—the call went immediately to a voicemail message telling the caller to contact someone else in the Rome bureau.

He fired off an email to Hamblyn instead, asking him to get in touch, then checked the time and put in a call to Marianne Tolman. After a moment, someone answered, possibly the second maid he'd encountered the previous week.

"Good morning, could I speak with Marianne Tolman, please?"

"May I ask who's calling?"

"Sure, it's Foster Treherne."

There was a lengthy pause, and then the voice came back, saying, "I'm sorry, Mr. Treherne, but Mrs. Tolman is at a retreat in New Mexico and can't be reached."

"I see. And when will she be back?"

"I couldn't say right now. She usually spends several weeks down there."

"Okay. Thanks for your time."

He called Josefin Widegren, but her phone just rang continuously without even going to voicemail. Then he looked and saw that he'd had an immediate "out of office" from Chris Hamblyn saying he was on vacation for three weeks—the same Chris Hamblyn who hadn't been able to spare the time to attend Charlie Treherne's funeral because of the busy political situation in Italy.

Foster went back and sat opposite Daniela, who was looking through the notebook. She glanced up.

"I hope you don't mind."

"Not at all. Can you read it? He had pretty crabbed handwriting."

"I can read it." She smiled. "Makes me feel envious somehow."

He nodded, glad it wasn't just him, but said, "On the other hand, it suddenly seems very difficult for me to reach any of the people in that photograph."

"I don't get it. Why, what's going on?"

"Two things, I guess. Firstly, the people in the picture are the members of something called the Piranesi Society, a group that formed at Bologna University—they visited ancient cemeteries and monastery libraries, that kind of thing, searching for arcane knowledge—"

"So that's what the references are in the notebook. I'm such a geek—I love that kind of thing."

"Yeah, it sounds pretty cool, but my dad's journal suggests there were some tensions, too."

"As you'd expect in a close group of friends." She latched on to something else and said, "You mentioned there were two things going on."

"You're here in an unofficial capacity, right?" She nodded, intrigued, and Foster said, "Professor Dorn suggested . . . No, that's too strong. There were some buttons torn from my dad's shirt and slight abrasions on the chest, suggestive of him maybe being in a scuffle. If he hadn't been alone that day, Dorn said his companion would at least have had some questions to answer."

"But . . . he *was* alone?"

"Originally, all of them had been planning to go on that trip. In the end it was just Charlie and Giorgio Pichler." He pointed out Giorgio in the picture. "Giorgio got sick and didn't walk with him the final day, but none of the three people I spoke with claim to know anything about what happened to Giorgio, so I haven't been able to ask him about it. They also failed to mention Gregory Tolman to me, and he's the person my dad seemed to have the most issues with."

Daniela nodded, but sounded measured as she said, "So they're covering something up, but it's still a big leap from there to concluding that one or more of them set out to hurt your dad or even killed him. It could be something completely different that they're trying to keep a lid on."

"Like what?"

She shrugged. "Who knows? Drugs? Or . . . maybe they were stealing artefacts from some of these places they were visiting, something like that."

Thinking back to Josefin Widegren telling him about dripping blood onto the von Stosch tomb, Foster could believe that drugs and esoteric larceny might easily have played a part in their activities. And maybe some of them would want to conceal those activities now; but despite Daniela's skepticism, Foster remained convinced that the Piranesi Society had been involved with his father's death in one way or another.

"You could be right, it could be nothing—"

"But you need to know." He nodded and she smiled sympathetically and said, "Is this all you have, this notebook and one photograph?"

"No, I have a whole bunch of photographs upstairs."

"Could I see?"

"Sure, although I can't imagine them telling you very much."

"You never know, there might be something there that gives us a clue. I mean, until you looked at this picture, you didn't know about Gregory Tolman. So who knows what else is hidden?"

"Then let's go and take a look." He pointed at her mug. "But I'd bring your coffee with you—my skills in that department are pretty unreliable."

She smiled, picking up her coffee and standing, looking eager. And Foster understood that because he felt it, too. They'd both been envious of the Piranesi Society in one way or another—of the camaraderie, of the romantic searches for obscure knowledge—and here they were about to search through the remnants of that society, looking for some obscure knowledge of their own.

Twenty-Two

When they got to the apartment she glanced briefly at the table full of clutter, but then drifted around the room looking at the paintings.

Finally she turned to face him and said, "I don't recognize any of these."

"They're all by the other members of The New Painters, which probably looks like guilt, but I genuinely liked them all, and it kind of reminds me of . . . well, lots of things." He pointed to a male nude. "That one's by Polly Carmichael."

"Your ex-girlfriend?" He nodded. "She was good. Were you the model?"

"No." He laughed, because the guy was more muscled and sculpted than Foster had ever been—it was actually from pictures of a photoshoot she'd found online. "We never sat for each other."

She started to drift back toward him as she said, "Do you still use life models?"

"Yeah, usually just for practice, sometimes to sketch out ideas that I incorporate into the paintings later. I've never slept with any of them."

Teasing, she said, "Thank you for sharing."

He held up his hands, admitting it was a strange thing to say. "My last girlfriend, Nele, got very jealous about models, and I have no doubt there are artists who still behave like that, but, you know . . . I'll just shut up now."

She laughed, but there was warmth in her eyes. He liked her. It was too soon to know if she liked him or if there might be anything there, but it mattered to Foster that she didn't think badly of him.

Daniela looked down at the table, but the first thing she picked up was a note that he recognized immediately—it was the Comic Sans note he'd intended to give to Sigrid before he'd changed his mind. He'd dropped it on the table and forgotten about it.

"That's not my dad's, it's mine. I must have just left it there."

Daniela's brow creased with a frown as she said, "Is this a threat of some kind, something about your next show?"

"It's been dealt with. We know who it is, and it's not a threat."

"It reads like a threat to me." Foster shrugged and she said, "Do you get a lot of this kind of thing?"

"Some. This particular one is also linked to The New Painters, but it's really not that interesting."

"I'd like to hear about it anyway."

"Another time maybe?"

"Okay. I don't want to pry." She laughed again—she laughed easily and he liked that too. "Says the woman who's just about to pry into the dark recesses of your family history."

She sat down and started looking through the photographs at one end of the table, lingering over them, pointing out the young Gregory Tolman in some of the shots.

Finally she leaned back in her chair and said, "It doesn't really tell us much. Makes me envious, though. These pictures are kind of how I imagined college would be, but it wasn't, not really."

"Where did you go?"

"Georgetown, which was great." She waved her hand at the array of photographs. "It just wasn't this."

"I know what you mean."

"Goldsmiths must have been fun, though? I mean, London at that age has to be fun."

Even now, after a decade of fame, it surprised him that people knew simple details like that about him, the ballast of conversations with new friends—*where did you go to college, what did your parents do, where did you grow up?*

"Yeah, we had fun. But we were all so driven and focused. You know, we were ambitious to make our mark like the YBAs did all those years ago. Looking back now, I'm amazed how many of our late-night conversations revolved around that subject."

She looked momentarily at the paintings hanging nearby and said, "That must have been hard for some of the others, then, when it didn't happen for them."

He sensed she was shifting attention back to the Comic Sans note, so he simply nodded and gestured to the photographs again, saying, "You have to remember with these, they were all postgraduates when they were at Bologna, in their mid-twenties, not that much younger than we are now. In fact, my dad actually says in his journal that the Piranesi Society is exactly what he'd hoped to find at Yale but hadn't. So I guess they were pretty knowing about creating this idealized student existence."

She nodded and picked up a photograph of Lucy, looking into the camera with a wry smile, the ochre of a colonnaded building forming the backdrop.

"Your mother was beautiful. I mean, your dad was a good-looking guy, but she was incredibly beautiful."

She was still staring intently at the photograph as she spoke, a hint of sadness in her voice and in her eyes. He'd never thought of his mother as anything except dead. The only thing he'd ever truly known about her as a living person was that she'd killed herself and left him alone. Yes, on a purely aesthetic level he could see she'd

140

been beautiful, but not like the beauty of Daniela Herrera, sitting in front of him now, a beauty that wasn't just on the surface.

Foster said, "I've never felt any connection to her at all."

"I can understand that. The same with your dad?"

"No. I did feel a connection with him. Maybe because I always thought he'd come back." She smiled, sympathetic, and put the photograph back with the others, and as the thought came to him, Foster said, "Would you like to go to dinner?"

"Sure," she said. "When did you have in mind?"

"Right now." He looked at his watch. "I realize it's early, but I haven't eaten yet. There are some great little places in the neighborhood."

"Then we should go." She laughed. "I thought you were asking me on a date!"

"I wouldn't know how. I don't think I've ever been on a date, not in any usual way, you know, like they do in movies and things."

She looked shocked. "You've never been on a date? You never said to a girl, 'You wanna come see a movie or go to dinner'—apart from just now—nothing like that?" He shook his head. "And so I don't even need to ask if you've ever used a dating app."

"No. No, I . . . It just always happened, you know. I haven't led a very ordinary life."

"You're telling me." She pushed herself away from the table and stood. "And I'm envious of that too."

He nodded, accepting the point, the gentle reminder that he'd been luckier than most people, for all the tragedy at the beginning of his life. And he was smiling, too, because he had not asked her out on a date, but she'd thought he had, and she'd said yes anyway.

Twenty-Three

They went to his favorite local Italian restaurant, and as they ate, now that the subject had been broached, she told him about her own life, how she'd had a boyfriend back in Washington but they'd broken up. She'd been single for the eighteen months she'd been in Berlin, despite a handful of first dates with coworkers.

In turn, he told her about Nele and the reasons it hadn't worked, and Daniela said, "Was she an artist too?"

"No, she was still at college, studying fashion design." He could see her making an immediate assumption, so he said, "She was twenty-eight—they stay at college much later here, and she'd been traveling for a few years in her early twenties."

"So she had less excuse making demands of you. Different if she had her own career to focus on. That said, can't be easy if you're both artists, either."

He sensed Daniela might be pulling the conversation back to the subject of the threatening letters, but it was averted when the waiter came to the table to clear their plates. And it was nearly another hour, through which the conversation flowed freely, before she came back to something that had clearly been on her mind since being up in the loft.

"Tell me about the letter, the one with the cartoon typeface. You said it had something to do with The New Painters."

"I also said it wasn't very interesting." She stared back at him, a wry smile but unyielding. "I get a lot of this—so does anyone in the public eye. Those particular letters have been coming for a while. Sigrid looked into it, and it turns out they're being sent by Polly Carmichael's husband, either on her behalf or he's just acting alone."

Daniela's eyes opened wide. They were dark and deep.

"But that's just . . . it's just bitter. It's not your fault that you've been so successful."

"True, but that's from my perspective. I think you'd have to understand a little more of how it all went down at the time to get their point of view."

He realized as he was talking that he wasn't just thinking about Polly, but the other ten artists in The New Painters, too—a few had gone on to get a career out of it, but none had come close to the success Foster had enjoyed.

"So tell me."

He nodded, took a sip of wine. "We were all pretty close, and we'd been planning The New Painters for probably half our time at Goldsmiths. You know, it was a big dream, for all of us. Then the show finally happened and I got taken on by a gallery right away, sold a couple of paintings, all on the first day. Then the gallery released some details about my background—the father who disappeared in the Alps, the grief-stricken mother who killed herself—and that got the wider press and media interested. In the first interview I did, I talked about Polly and some of the others, and afterward, the gallerist told me I should only talk about myself, that success was fickle and I had to grasp it. And I believed him, and it terrified me, because we'd all been dreaming about this kind of success for so long."

"That's perfectly natural."

"Yeah, I guess. The newspaper didn't use any of the stuff about the others anyway, just talked about me. And from then on, so did I. I wanted what they were offering, and I wanted it for me more than I wanted it for anyone else. By the end of the first week, everything I had in the show had sold and the art world was going crazy for me. So . . . I didn't exactly throw the others under the bus, but I didn't help them get on it either. And I still occasionally think about whether I could have done it differently. Whatever, Polly left me a couple of months later."

Shocked, Daniela said, "Because you were a success?"

"I presume so."

"You presume? Didn't you ask her?"

"No. She said she was leaving. And . . . I said that was okay."

"You didn't fight, didn't try to get her to stay?"

She seemed incredulous.

"No. She said she wanted to leave."

"That's what she *said*. Doesn't mean it's what she *wanted*." Daniela sipped at her wine, but then shook her head in disbelief, as if she still couldn't get to grips with the way he'd acted all those years ago. "Did you love her?"

"Yeah, I loved her. Honestly, I was distracted by the sudden success, but I loved her. It hurt when she left."

Daniela leaned back in her seat, dumbfounded, staring at him, and then she seemed struck by some profound understanding. "It's how you defend yourself, isn't it? I've seen this before. Your whole life, in one way or another, people have left you, so you deal with it by disconnecting, pretending it's entirely out of your control." She appeared to have second thoughts, then. "Sorry, that was a pretty crappy thing to say."

"No, it wasn't." She said she'd seen it before, but Foster had also been accused of it before, and at some level he knew it was the truth. "You have to accept it's been the one constant in my life. People leave."

"They do, for all kinds of reasons, and sometimes they have no choice. But sometimes people stay, Foster. Sometimes, despite everything, people stay."

◆ ◆ ◆

It was still only early evening when they got back to the studio, lightheaded with wine after walking through the cool dusk. The others had all left for the day. Daniela stopped inside the door and looked around, apparently mesmerized by the silence in much the same way Foster was when he was here on his own.

She said, "It's like you can hear the building breathing. You must love being in the studio when it's like this."

"I do. You wanna take a look?"

She shook her head, and took his hand in hers and pulled him gently toward the elevator, and once the door shut behind them and the elevator started to move, she kissed him. Foster closed his eyes as they kissed and took in the taste and scent of her and the feel of her body against his hands, and he felt—deep below the adrenaline and the excitement—a profound sense of peace.

She led him to the bedroom and then the excitement of being there with her drowned out everything else, but afterward, as they lay together, the sense of peace and contentment returned. He couldn't know so soon, and yet he felt it so keenly—that he wanted to be with this woman, wanted to be with her in a way he'd never felt with Nele, or maybe not with anyone since Polly.

Much later, as Daniela slept, he got up and went to the studio and worked on the glacial canvas, shifting the grays and whites across the landscape, and still the feeling of peace persisted within his core. And it wasn't until hours later that he stood back and tried to see where the figure belonged in this painting.

He thought through a few options, but none of them seemed right, and in the end he shook his head and said quietly, "Where are you?"

No answer came readily, and he cleaned up and left.

Twenty-Four

Daniela was already up, sitting at the table looking over the contents of his dad's college room. A mug of coffee sat on the table in front of her. She was wearing a plain white T-shirt.

She smiled and stood, saying, "I made coffee—would you like some? Oh, and I borrowed one of your T-shirts." She came over and kissed him. Her mouth tasted of toothpaste. She wasn't much shorter than him, and as she walked over to the counter he noticed with a stirring in his blood that the T-shirt didn't do much to cover her.

She came back with a mug of coffee and placed it on the table, and Foster said, "Thanks. I don't know if that's how dates normally work—"

She pulled a face and said, "It's not how dates normally work with me! Trust me, I don't go falling into bed with men every two minutes."

"Then I'm doubly grateful."

She kissed him again, but pulled away and went and sat down. Foster sat opposite her and nursed the coffee, feeling the chill now that the sun had risen.

"Do you have work today?"

"I'm off for the rest of the week. But I'll need to go back to my apartment." She waited a beat before adding, "Do you always work at night?"

He nodded, but said, "Sometimes I work around the clock, but yeah, usually late at night." He felt a low-level nervous excitement, wondering if, even after one night, she was trying to figure out if this would work. "I realize that doesn't make me ideal boyfriend material. Nele wanted me to paint during the day, like Magritte."

"Then maybe she should have dated Magritte." Foster laughed and she said, "We're grown-ups, I'm sure we can work something out. Like, I could just stay over at weekends. I mean, I wanna see where this might go. If you do."

"Absolutely." Despite himself, he yawned. "I need to sleep."

She nodded and put her hand on his. "So sleep. I'll go and I'll come back."

He went into the bedroom, pulled off his clothes, and crashed onto the bed. Daniela went into the bathroom, but he'd fallen into a deep untroubled sleep before she came out. And when he woke again he thought he'd only slept a short while because he could still smell fresh coffee, but he felt rested and when he checked the time it was just before midday.

He showered and went through to find her sitting at the table again. She was dressed in different clothes, the only real indication that she'd been home. She smiled, but looked troubled somehow.

"Good morning."

"Morning," said Foster, his expression quizzical, asking her what was wrong.

"You should get some coffee and sit down. It might not . . . well, it probably doesn't have any connection, but I found something kind of disturbing."

He poured himself a coffee and sat opposite her. Daniela picked up an envelope and pulled out the letter inside.

"I guess this is from an old college friend, someone called Marcus. It was sent to your dad in Bologna. *Hope you're having much fun in Bologna, but bet you're not having this much fun. A reminder of more riotous times. Remember? I know she didn't."*

"Yeah, I saw that letter. Didn't make much sense, still doesn't."

"So I'm guessing you didn't notice the snapshot." She reached back into the envelope and pulled a photograph free, handing it to him.

It was an old Polaroid snap, and Foster felt his heart sink as soon as he looked at it. A young woman was pictured lying on a bed. Only her upper body was visible in the picture, but that part was naked, and the girl was clearly unconscious. Two young men were either side of her, wearing T-shirts, grinning at the camera and giving a thumbs-up, as if posing with some trophy kill. One of them was Charlie Treherne.

Foster dropped the photograph on the table, then reached out and turned it over, disturbed by the sight of his father's triumphant grin. He'd heard repeatedly that his dad had been a lot of fun, and until now he'd seen him as a victim, with the truth being buried in some sinister plot by the rest of the Piranesi Society.

All of that could still be true, but this picture hinted at something else, and now he remembered that comment Marianne Tolman had made—saying that Charlie had always appeared on the verge of doing something he shouldn't do.

Foster noticed writing on the back of the Polaroid and picked it up again. In faint blue ink he could just see *Lisa K 3-0!* He didn't even want to know what the numbers referred to, but he felt an almost visceral need to find out who this woman was, even though he knew that, too, was probably the wrong thing to do.

Daniela had been silent, but said now, "Look, this is the kind of thing that, if your dad were still alive and in some elevated position, it could destroy him. The thing is, I'm guessing this was the mid-eighties, and I'm not excusing it, but it was a different culture. I mean, there were guys at college with me who still didn't get it— posting stuff like this on the web, revenge porn, you name it—but back then it was probably much more the norm, or at least more common."

Foster shook his head, grateful that she was tying herself in knots to protect the memory of his father, but also knowing that she couldn't believe it. "Maybe it was a different culture, but even then, I guarantee there were a lot of guys who wouldn't act like this, and we don't even know what this was. I mean, '3-0'? Do we even want to know what that means?"

"Okay, I agree." She looked along the table, taking in the full contents of Charlie's Bologna room in one sweep. "But look, even if this picture represents who he truly was, it doesn't excuse what might have happened to him in Switzerland. These friends from Bologna are covering something up, and you have every right to find out what it is."

He nodded. He thought of trying to call Josefin Widegren again, but he needed to know more first, about the boy his father had been in that Polaroid. Daniela had spoken the truth—no matter who he'd been, he hadn't deserved what had happened to him on the Handeck Glacier, but Foster still needed to know.

"I'm just going down to the office. Back in a minute. Maybe we could get . . ."

"Breakfast?"

She smiled and it eased his disquiet immediately.

"Sure, I can get breakfast, you can get lunch." He leaned over, kissed her. "I'll be back soon."

He took the elevator, and once the usual greetings were out of the way and approving comments about Daniela had been made, he said, "Maja, could you get in touch with Benny, ask him to send over the other boxes that were with the one he already sent? I think one's marked 'Yale' and one's marked 'Bennington', but just ask him to send them all over."

"I'm on it."

"Great." He looked at Natsuko's desk and spotted another Comic Sans note, but pointed and shook his head. "You can file that, but seriously, I don't think we need worry about it."

"I guessed as much," said Natsuko. "But you asked about Gregory Tolman. We haven't found much yet, but we did discover he'll be at the party the Bureau of Educational and Cultural Affairs is throwing for the Biennale in a few weeks."

"Was I invited?"

She nodded. "You declined."

She said it as if stating the obvious—he didn't like being around other artists.

"Could you let them know I'm unexpectedly available and would love to come?"

"Of course, and I'm sure they'll be happy. You want me to book rooms at the Ca' Sagredo?"

"Please. You don't mind coming along? It's short notice."

"It's Venice, Foster."

"When you put it like that." He looked around the room, a feeling that he'd forgotten something. "Do I have anything planned for today?"

"No, all clear."

"Good, I'm heading out to lunch with Daniela." He ignored their smiles, but was touched by how invested the three of them seemed to be in his happiness. "But I want to keep on top of this Gregory Tolman business. I need to know everything about him before we meet."

He left them then and went back up to Daniela, but he was uneasy without being sure why. Maybe it was simply that Polaroid making him fearful. He was still convinced his father had been the victim of a crime and that the surviving members of the Piranesi Society—Gregory Tolman chief among them—were concealing the truth of their part in it. But not all victims were innocent, and Charlie Treherne, it seemed, really had been a young man always on the edge of doing something he shouldn't.

Twenty-Five

Over the next few days Foster and Daniela fell into a routine together. It concerned him now and then—how natural it felt, how easily their lives were intertwining, how attached he was becoming to her being there.

He had never liked having people in the studio with him, but on the third night she came down while he was painting, unable to sleep, and asked if she could watch. She curled up on the paint-spattered couch and looked on in silence and eventually fell asleep.

When he finished painting, he sat on the floor in front of the couch and watched her, and he felt a fear he had never felt before, that he was investing too much too soon, that this could not last. He was a hostage, for the first time ever—at least, to someone living.

And then the next morning, the boxes arrived from New York. Apart from two more unsuccessful attempts to reach Josefin Widegren by phone, Foster hadn't given much thought to his father for a couple of days, and initially he was tempted to leave it that way and put the boxes to one side.

It was Daniela who said, "We should look through them one at a time. Start with Bennington—that was his high school, right?"

"Yeah, mine too."

"So we can take them upstairs and look through them. The sooner we do it, the sooner it's done."

They took them to the apartment and emptied the contents of the Bennington box across the table, just as he had done with the one from Bologna. It wasn't especially revealing of anything except the period—the late 1970s—that his father had been there.

Bennington hadn't been coed back then, so there were lots of photographs of groups of boys posing together, or in dorm rooms. The haircuts, the posters visible on the walls, even the grain of the photographs seemed imbued with the seedy tint of the seventies. Charlie didn't stand out in the photographs which featured him— just another ungainly adolescent.

There were no pictures of the grand buildings themselves, and without them, there wasn't even anything here to remind Foster of his own school days.

Daniela sighed heavily, and said, "There are plenty of photographs of kids smiling, but it still looks kind of miserable somehow. Is this how it was when you were there?"

Foster shook his head. "This could've been a hundred years ago, nothing like the place I went to. We had girls, for one thing." He laughed, realizing how that sounded. "But it was actually a pretty cool place. And you're right, these do look miserable."

They gathered everything together and put it back into the box, then emptied the Yale box across the table, and, just looking at the contents, it was possible to see the epochal shift into the '80s. There were tickets to see bands, flyers for club and society events around college, postcards and letters, and a much bigger variety of photographs now.

Foster looked through one after another, a lot of them in what appeared to be party-type situations. His dad was coming into his own, clearly on the way from being the adolescent in the

Bennington photographs to the more poised and confident young man in those from Bologna.

And thankfully, there weren't any more of him grinning like a creep over a naked girl. If anything, there were quite a few pictures of him with girls who looked comfortable with him, sitting on his lap, arms draped across him.

Daniela was looking through letters, and said now, "Oh, this is interesting. This must be from a girl he knew from home, someone called Natalie. She says, *Please, please, please, help get my cousin into the Wig & Pen—I'll be eternally grateful.*"

"What's the Wig & Pen?"

"Sounds like a society. Yale has a whole bunch of them." She took her phone and searched, scrolling through the results.

"You mean like a frat house?"

Without looking up, she said, "No, they're separate from fraternities, and you can be a member of both. Okay, here we go . . ." She studied the screen of her phone in silence for a second or two. "Okay, despite the ancient-sounding name, the Wig & Pen was founded only in 1951. In the late sixties and seventies it developed a reputation for scandalous parties and dangerous pranks. The society was banned in 1991, although there have been several failed attempts to resurrect it. Doesn't say what triggered the banning, though."

"My father was already dead by then, anyway. But it probably goes some way to explaining that Polaroid."

She nodded, put the letter aside, and opened another, and Foster went back to looking through the photographs. He was just thinking it was strange that the girl who'd appeared naked in the Polaroid didn't feature in any of the more regular photos, when Daniela spoke again.

"Was that girl Lisa K?"

"Yeah."

"Then I think we might know who she is. Our friend Natalie seems to be a mine of information. According to her, *Lisa Kinneston has always been a first-class bitch, so that doesn't surprise me at all.* She doesn't say what 'that' refers to, but she's obviously replying to something your dad said in a previous letter." She smiled then, holding up the letter. "It's so weird. I mean, this is so recent, our parents' generation, and they wrote letters to each other like it was, I don't know, the nineteenth century or something."

"Lucky for us, though. Imagine trying to track these people down from their emails and messages."

He got up and fetched his laptop, opening it and searching for "Lisa Kinneston" and "Yale." He got plenty of image hits, including a good number that appeared to have been posted on various social media sites by people being nostalgic about their college days.

Foster turned the screen so that Daniela could see it too, then got the Polaroid and placed it alongside. He kept getting distracted, his gaze lured again and again to his dad's jubilant face, but then he spotted a picture of three girls on the screen and said, "Is that her?"

"I think so."

He opened it up and now the resemblance was even clearer. Even better, it had been posted on Instagram by one of the other girls in the picture, and the caption read, *Happy memories of Yale Law.*

Daniela spotted it too and said, "So maybe she's a lawyer."

Foster searched again, "Lisa Kinneston, Attorney," and got a hit for a law firm in New York City. She was a partner, and on her profile page she looked sleeker and almost more youthful in some way than in the picture with her two friends from Yale Law.

Daniela said, "What do you want to do now?"

"Call her, I guess."

"And ask her . . . 'Why do I have a snap of you naked and unconscious with my dad and his friend?'"

She had a point. Lisa Kinneston probably had a lot of happy memories of her time at Yale, and it was highly unlikely she'd want to have someone like Foster dredging up considerably less happy ones.

He wasn't even sure what it was that he wanted to know. Did he want to hear that this snap represented a colossal one-off error of judgment by his father, or that it more truly represented who he was? And would either revelation make any difference to what had happened subsequently in Europe? Either way, he had to know.

Twenty-Six

It was Friday afternoon and Foster was determined to have this out of the way by the weekend. Daniela had gone back to her apartment, but would be spending the weekend with him before returning to the office on Monday—what she called a trial run for how this would work in the future. How it "would" work, not how it "might."

He called Lisa Kinneston's firm at 10 a.m. New York time and asked to speak to her, giving his own name. The receptionist put him on hold, then told him that Lisa Kinneston was in a meeting. He gave his name again, and his number, and asked if she could call him back.

He ended the call, imagining she was just one more person who didn't want to speak to him about his father, but within five minutes his phone rang.

He answered and a voice said, "Foster Treherne?"

"Speaking."

"I have Lisa Kinneston on the line for you. Please hold." A second later, Lisa Kinneston said, "Good morning, Mr. Treherne, what can I do for you?" Her voice had a measured quality about it, full of traps for people on the wrong side of her interrogations, but probably reassuring for her own clients.

"Hello. Please call me Foster. And is it Lisa or Ms. Kinneston?"

"Lisa's fine," she said, a hint of impatience.

"Great. I was hoping you might fill in some blanks for me, Lisa. You may not remember, but you were at Yale with my father."

She sounded amused as she said, "Oh, Mr. Treherne, naturally I know who you are, but I would not have been returning this call if it hadn't been for who your father was. I remember the news story when he disappeared, and I saw the more recent one when he was found. My condolences."

"Thanks. So you were friends?"

There was a pause, just the briefest moment, but discernible all the same.

"No, I wouldn't say that. We moved in the same circles. I'm not saying we *disliked* each other, just that we weren't particularly close."

"So you had no . . . How can I put this? You had no complaint against him?"

"You sound like you have a point, Mr. Treherne—how about getting to it?"

He smiled to himself, impressed by the no-nonsense tone.

"Okay. After my father's body was found, I looked through some boxes of his possessions. Among them, I found a Polaroid, featuring you and my father and one other person."

"I presume you wouldn't be mentioning it if it weren't a compromising photograph."

"It is, though I think more for him and his friend than for you. The picture only shows you from the waist up, but you are topless, and also apparently unconscious. The other two are clothed, grinning at the camera, thumbs up."

There was another pause, then a sigh, and she said, "Marcus—that's the other boy in the picture—he's told me more than once of its existence. Maybe I should be happy that it's surfaced where it has. I imagine you have no plans to publish it?"

157

"Absolutely not. I intend to destroy it, unless you—"

She laughed, an edge of bitterness about it, and said, "No, trust me, I'm quite happy for you to destroy it. And of course you would wish to destroy it. Maybe it says something about how society has changed that at the time that picture would have destroyed my reputation, whereas now it would destroy Marcus and Charlie's. I wouldn't want that."

Did that suggest some sympathy for his dad, some sense that the photograph seemed worse than it was?

"Do you mind telling me about it?"

"Surely it should be obvious that I didn't know much about it." She sighed heavily, then added, "They were both in the Wig & Pen—an all-male society, obviously. There was something rather exciting about that. The Wig & Pen had a reputation for being the most riotous society, and for throwing great parties. In hindsight, those parties *were* great, but they were not without their dangers, for female students in particular."

"What kind of dangers?"

"Really? I can't imagine I need to spell it out. I think in my case I got off pretty lightly. I went, I drank, I . . . lost consciousness and woke up naked under a coat. Naturally, I have no idea what happened to me in between, though I'm pretty confident I wasn't raped."

Her matter-of-fact tone momentarily left Foster without a reply.

"I . . ." He made an effort to focus on what was important, to him at least. "Lisa, I have to tell you, that picture made me feel sick, to think that my dad was the kind of guy who . . ."

She gave him the opportunity to finish the sentence, then when he didn't, she said, "Charlie wasn't malicious, Mr. Treherne. He was just always looking for thrills, you know, and so it never mattered that what he was doing was . . . Well, it was a different era."

"That's hardly an excuse."

"I'm not excusing his or anyone else's behavior. These guys weren't cruel, they weren't violent—and there were plenty of men around who *were* like that—but they treated women in a certain way, and they were smart enough to know it was wrong. It's just that society wasn't advanced enough to hold them to account for it. Sadly, recent events suggest it still isn't, not entirely."

"I'm sorry anyway, sorry it happened to you."

"You have nothing to apologize for, Foster." He noticed it was the first time she'd used his first name. "I know from the press that you weren't even born when he disappeared, and for all his faults—and he did have faults—it's a tragedy that his life was cut short like that."

"I guess so." Though at the moment, Foster was imagining the Polaroid snap emerging if his father had lived, and how it would have soured things between them. "And I appreciate you calling me back."

"I'm glad to have spoken to you. And I do have to jump on another call now, but there's one last thing I'd like to tell you. From what I remember of him, I could imagine Charlie being involved in . . . in whatever happened that night. But I also recall that I vaguely regained consciousness at one point, just enough to see that it was also Charlie who covered me with that coat. And I've wondered about that all this time."

"I see."

"Good. You've lost so much already. Don't judge the person he would have become by the person he was at twenty. And now I do have to go. Good to speak with you, Mr. Treherne."

"And you. Thank you."

Foster put the phone down and sat there without moving for a minute or so, paralyzed by too much information. Most of all, he wished he could get in touch with his dad's former correspondent,

Natalie, to tell her Lisa Kinneston was not "a first-class bitch"—she wasn't anything of the sort.

Foster was also struggling to synchronize these different aspects of his father's personality. He was someone who, at the very least, would find it amusing to pose for a photograph with a girl who was naked and unconscious. Yet he was also someone who'd then cover that girl with a coat. Briefly, Foster wanted to believe the photo had been the full extent of his dad's involvement in whatever had gone on at that party, but the doubts were too strong . . .

Without thinking about it, Foster called Josefin Widegren's number again, and once more it rang without an answer. He ended the call and stared at the phone. Don't judge him by the person he'd been at twenty, that's what Lisa Kinneston had said, but how else was Foster to judge him when he'd only lived five more years?

Foster had been part of The New Painters at twenty-one, and maybe he had been ambitious to the point of ruthlessness back then. He would have liked to have helped the others, but there was no question that his own art and his own career would come first. And he was still that same person—success had rendered those traits invisible, but they were still there.

He called again, but this time, almost immediately, the call was answered and Josefin Widegren's incredulous voice said, "You really don't give up, do you, Mr. Treherne?"

"No, I don't." In finally picking up the call, she'd caught him off guard and it took him a moment to remind himself why he was calling. "I wouldn't have disturbed you if it weren't important, Jo, but I need to see you again. There's something I need to discuss."

He was dreading that she would ask him what it was over the phone, because he wasn't even sure what was most important now—what they were covering up or what kind of person Charlie had really been.

But she simply said, "Very well, when would be good for you?"

He heard the elevator stirring behind him and guessed it was Daniela coming back.

"How about early next week? Monday or Tuesday?"

"Monday afternoon would be fine. Any time after lunch. I'll be here."

He thanked her and ended the call, but his focus was returning now. It wasn't that she'd been away; she'd been avoiding his calls, just as Chris Hamblyn and Marianne Tolman had. That only reinforced his original suspicion—that they were hiding something, the key to which was probably in the airbrushing of Gregory Tolman from that group photograph.

The elevator door opened and he stood to meet Daniela as she stepped into the loft carrying a small bag.

"See, I came back!"

He smiled and kissed her and held on to her for a second or two.

When he broke away she looked him in the eye and said, "Everything okay?"

"Oh, I finally got through to Josefin—I'm seeing her Monday afternoon. But I also spoke with Lisa Kinneston."

Her eyes opened wide. "Was that wise? How did she take it? I mean . . ."

He shrugged. "She kind of knew about the photo. She was at a Wig & Pen party, got drunk, woke up naked under a coat. Said she was certain she wasn't raped, but even if that's true, it was still . . ."

Daniela dropped the bag. "And your dad was involved?"

"Yeah. She suggested it was part of the culture, among that particular group anyway. It was a weird conversation. She was also pretty defensive of my dad, said he wasn't mean, said she had a vague memory that it was Charlie who covered her with the coat."

Daniela took a deep breath and said, "Wow."

"Yeah, she also said I shouldn't judge him by who he was at twenty."

"Well, I disagree with her on that. In my experience, a douche-bag at twenty stays a douchebag." Foster nodded, acknowledging to himself that someone who was ruthless and self-serving at twenty stayed that way. "But that really is weird, about him covering her with a coat. I wonder if he felt guilty, or if he just . . . I don't know, is it possible he felt some compassion after the fact?"

"That would be almost worse, like these sex offenders who treat their victims with tenderness afterward, like it's a consensual relationship." Daniela visibly shuddered, then smiled and said, "Let's talk about something else."

"Okay, in other dad-related news, Josefin has been there all along, just not answering my calls. She's seeing me because I ground her down, not because she wants to help."

"Interesting. Suggests you're right about them trying to cover something up." She smiled. "Change the subject."

"We could go and eat?"

"Better. Or how about we go out and buy ingredients and eat here?"

"Sounds like a plan."

He kissed her again, losing himself. Everything else fell away in her presence, for the time being at least. As long as she was here, it was almost as if Charlie had never been found and the glacier had remained undisturbed, a fantasy almost as appealing as those he'd entertained in his childhood, of his father's triumphant return.

THIS IS ART NOW—
THE BLOG WITH THE SCOOP ON THE VISUAL

June 22, 2011

Polly Carmichael: I don't want to get into a blame game.

Jenny Says: But you must have your suspicions, about the way he became famous, the way he courted the media to push his own work rather than The New Painters as a concept.

PC: Look, naturally, I feel like he used us. A part of me even respects that level of ruthlessness. Foster looked out for himself and it's worked for him so far, so good luck with that.

JS: You don't think his art merits the success he's had?

PC: I didn't say that. Look, I didn't agree to this interview to spend the whole time talking about Foster Treherne.

Twenty-Seven

The traffic was much the same as he remembered, the sky an identical pristine blue, but when Foster stepped out of the car at Josefin Widegren's house he noticed the mercury had climbed a good way since his last visit. Jo once more came to meet him, once again wearing an outfit that looked vaguely North African or Indian, this one made entirely from white linen.

"So lovely to see you again, Foster." She hugged him as if they were old friends. "Let's walk around to the gazebo."

She took him by the arm, no less oblivious to the driver than she had been the previous time. When they got to the gazebo she left Foster and went into the house. He sat listening—to the faint sound of laughter somewhere on a nearby beach, to the gentle put-put of a small boat far off. There was no breeze at all, the air throbbing with heat.

He sat there like that for fifteen minutes before Jo came out again, carrying a tray.

"I don't think you cared so much for my iced tea, so I thought I might have more luck with my coffee."

He smiled, but didn't respond until she'd poured him a cup, then said, "Thanks." He took a dutiful sip, expecting the worst but finding it good. "That's beautiful."

"Don't sound so surprised." She finished pouring her own. "Blue Mountain. But I don't think you came here to discuss my coffee." As she said this, she glanced at the envelope he'd placed on the table.

Foster nodded, took the envelope, and pulled out the familiar photograph. He placed it on the table in front of Jo.

"Okay, I was hoping you might tell me why Gregory Tolman doesn't appear in this picture."

She offered a bemused smile, then without looking down at the print, she said, "Greg was at Bologna, but not studying history. I think he was studying economics or something like that. We knew him, naturally, and we'd socialize with him on occasion, but Greg was never in the Piranesi Society."

"He wasn't in the Piranesi?"

"That's correct. I don't think I could have been any clearer about it."

"So then I have a different question." Foster took the original picture and placed it on top of the doctored one. "If he wasn't in the Piranesi Society, why is he in *this* picture?" She looked down this time, and smiled ruefully. Foster said, "I found it in my dad's papers."

"I see."

"It's why Chris Hamblyn pretended he couldn't remember Marianne's surname, and I presume it's why all three of you have been trying to avoid my calls this last week or so."

"I always thought that was foolish."

"Why was he removed from the picture?"

"You're a smart man, Foster, you must be able to work it out. You know who Gregory Tolman is, his standing, his political ambitions. The Piranesi was just a bit of fun, but there were rumors at the time that we were involved in all kinds of black magic rituals, nonsense like that. Even back then, talk like that made Greg nervous."

He remembered her lying to him, saying Giorgio had come up with the name for the society, and he saw the truth now.

"So it was Gregory Tolman who came up with the name, who was concerned about the possible impact on your future careers."

"Yes, it was Greg." Somewhere inside the house, a phone started to ring. Jo looked casually toward the sound, but seemed unperturbed. Foster thought of his own unanswered calls. "And I feel bad, because in covering up Greg's part in the society, we made you think there was something more suspicious, as if you didn't have enough to think about."

She looked genuinely apologetic, but that only served to concentrate Foster's mind, and to convince him there was still something going on here that they weren't telling him. In much the same way that putting Polly under surveillance was potentially a greater PR risk to Foster's career than the Comic Sans letters represented themselves, so the revelation of this attempt at a cover-up could damage Tolman much more than his membership of some stupid college society. There had to be something bigger that they were still trying to conceal.

But he could hardly accuse Jo of lying to him again. He thought of the Polaroid of his dad, that gleeful face, the thumbs-up above Lisa Kinneston's naked breasts, and had to resist the urge to shudder. But he also knew that focusing on Charlie's questionable behavior might be the best way of getting Jo to open up.

"What kind of man was my dad, truthfully?"

"I don't follow."

He finished his coffee and she leaned forward and filled the cup again.

"Thanks. I'll put it another way. You told me they weren't a couple as such, but you also made clear your group of friends

167

weren't casually sleeping with each other, swapping partners. So what was it?"

"They were very close. Your mother was so beautiful. Charlie paid her attention, made her laugh—he was funny—they spent a lot of time together." She refilled her own coffee cup. "That said, I never saw them as couple material, only as friends."

"I don't understand."

"What is there to understand, Foster? They went to a party together, got drunk, woke up in bed the next morning, no real memory of the night before, some embarrassment. And you were the result." She laughed, as if accusing him of being prudish. "Don't be so shocked. It may have been a one-night stand, but they *had been* friends."

Had been. Was that just the Swedish inflection in her voice, or did it suggest that their friendship hadn't survived the one-night stand? Was the fallout from it the reason the society had started to break apart, why only Charlie and Giorgio had ended up going on the trip to the Handeck Glacier?

Don't judge the person he would have become by the person he was at twenty.

"I know it was two months later, but did this incident have anything to do with the rest of you dropping out of the Handeck trip? Or had things already started to fall apart beforehand? I mean, in the pictures you're always together, yet it sounds from what you're saying that Charlie and Lucy went to this party on their own."

She shook her head, making a show of confusion at his line of questioning, and said, "I had a lot of work at the time. I'm not sure about Ham and Giorgio. Originally, Greg and Marianne had been going as well, but Marianne's father had a heart attack and she flew home. Greg flew home with her."

"Were they a couple by then?"

"No, not at that point. In fact, we all thought . . . But it was just the way Greg was. They'd known each other before Italy, you see, part of the same moneyed New York elite. So that's how Charlie and Lucy ended up going to the party on their own."

"But the one-night stand had nothing to do with the group breaking apart?"

"The group didn't break apart." She frowned. "You have me at a loss, Foster. I can tell that you're wanting something from me, but I don't know what."

He guessed what he was about to say would be inadmissible in a court, but he needed to say something that would break through Josefin's protective wall, even if it meant slandering his father unfairly.

"You know, I've been asking around, trying to find out about him. Turns out he was part of a society at Yale, the Wig & Pen. He ever mention that?" Josefin shook her head and he said, "It had a wild reputation, including what I guess we'd now call predatory sexual activity, getting girls drunk and . . . well, you know the kind of thing."

He was about to go on, but he didn't need to. Jo looked as if the energy had been knocked out of her, and Foster felt queasy with how cleanly he'd hit the target. She hadn't known about the Wig & Pen, but what he'd said had apparently struck a chord, resonating with the events she remembered from three decades ago.

She nodded her head, looking deep in thought, then said, "Marianne and Lucy were best friends, studying the same course. When Marianne got back from New York, Lucy told her she'd felt . . . strange that night, like someone had spiked her drink. It reinforced my own feeling."

"But you weren't at the party."

"No." The phone rang again inside the house, but Jo appeared not even to hear it. "As I told you, I had a lot of work, and I'd been in the library very late—I like to work at night even now—but I was just leaving when I saw them. At first I was going to say hello, but I thought of them being drunk, and I really couldn't be bothered with it. Maybe if I had . . ." She shrugged. "I hid behind one of the arches in the porticos, until they'd walked past. Lucy looked, I don't know . . . drunk, maybe, but in retrospect, it did look like more than that."

"And my dad?"

Josefin shook her head, frowning, and it could as easily have been at his use of the word "dad" as at the memory of that night.

"I don't think he was drunk at all. He was staggering a little, but only because she could hardly stand and he was holding her. And he had that look that he would get in his eyes—mischievous. I won't lie, that part of his psyche could be a lot of fun sometimes. He was an instigator, a disruptor. Life felt richer around him."

Foster was becoming impatient with her now, impatient with the various people who'd used descriptions like this to gloss over some more fundamental truth.

"But?"

"Yes—but! I can't lie. There was a dark side to him. I had no particular reason to think this way, but I always avoided being alone with him. Just a feeling, you know. And when Marianne told me what Lucy had said, my first thought was that it served her right, for being too trusting. I've had many years to regret that."

"You think he raped her."

She looked horrified. "I didn't say that. I . . . I don't know for sure what happened. They were *so* close, you know? Such good friends."

Foster laughed, a laugh that confused her.

"Okay, but you all suspected something bad had happened. And presumably you discussed it among yourselves."

"We girls did, and then Giorgio also."

Foster nodded. So the only person who'd gone to the Handeck Glacier with his father was the only man in the group they'd confided in.

"And it's why you all opted out of the Handeck trip."

"It's why I did. The others, it was just different things, and then tensions. Lucy wanted to go home anyway, to be in the care of their family doctor."

"What about Gregory Tolman?"

"I'm sorry?"

"I said, what about Gregory Tolman? Why did he drop out of the Handeck trip?"

She stared back at him, glassy-eyed, then picked up her coffee cup, but she looked at the black liquid inside and put it down again before saying, "Do you drink, Foster?"

"Yes."

"Would you mind going into the kitchen? You'll find a bottle of white wine in the fridge. You'll see the glasses in the cupboard on the left. I think I'd like a drink."

He got up without saying anything and walked toward the house. He could feel his blood beginning to spike with adrenaline, because of what he'd already heard, because of what he imagined he was about to hear. Josefin Widegren had more or less told him that his very existence was the result of date rape, and yet it was only the prospect of discussing Gregory Tolman's part in the subsequent events that had left her in need of a drink.

Twenty-Eight

Foster stepped through the glass doors into the cool stillness of the house's minimalist interior. It was the first time he'd been inside and it seemed out of keeping with Josefin's hippy dress sense and her past interest in esoterica—there was something crystalline and icy about this building.

He found the wine, found a corkscrew on the counter, and opened the bottle. The glasses took longer to locate, but when he walked out five or so minutes later, it looked as if Josefin hadn't moved a muscle since he'd left her.

She still sat vacantly as he placed the glasses on the table and poured for both of them, and didn't make eye contact even as she accepted one of the glasses.

She only looked at him and smiled sadly once he'd sat down again himself, then said, "I've always thought the problem with secrets is that they make it appear you have something to hide. And people fill in the blanks—the Piranesi was no different. I'm sure I don't need to tell you, but the artist Piranesi drew a lot of imagined and fantastical prisons, so rumors went around that we were into . . . S & M and things like that, all because Greg was worried about being associated with von Stosch."

Foster sipped his wine and found it dizzyingly refreshing against the heat of the afternoon. He immediately put the glass back on the table, determined not to drink too much. He wanted his thoughts clear.

"Why wasn't Greg on the trip to Handeck?"

"He was meant to go. I can't remember the reason he gave for backing out, but it wasn't odd or surprising. Everything felt like it was falling apart by then, people going their separate ways. Lucy had gone back to England. Ham was deeply involved with this awful Italian girl he was seeing. Marianne was trying to catch up on all the work she'd missed while her father was sick."

"So he didn't have any suspicions about what had happened between my mom and dad?"

She gave that odd grimace again, as if being reminded of Foster's parentage caused her some kind of discomfort, but it could have easily been in response to the question itself. She took a gulp of wine, and was already halfway down the glass.

"I don't think so. Yes, it's possible he had suspicions—he was very shocked by the news that they'd slept together. But then, after Charlie and Giorgio had been away for a few days already, Greg and I went for a drink. He mentioned that Marianne had confided in him, that Lucy thought Charlie might have slipped her a roofie. Greg sometimes had a prickly relationship with Charlie—I don't mind saying so—but he still didn't believe Charlie could have done something like that. I didn't like how quickly he was taking sides with another man over the word of a woman. Because Lucy had no reason at all to lie about it—none of us would have judged her for getting drunk or sleeping with Charlie." She took another sip of wine, then reached over for the bottle and poured herself some more. "So I told him what I'd seen that night."

"How did he respond?"

"He was shocked. None of us knew about this Pig & Pen society at Yale. Until you just mentioned it, I'd had no idea at all. We knew he was wild in his own way, but something like that—"

173

"Jo, you told me you avoided being alone with him."

That seemed to knock her back, and her features were downcast as she said, "That was just a feeling. I thought he might try something and I didn't want the hassle, but this was much worse—I don't think I ever imagined he could do things like that, particularly with Lucy."

Because they were "so close," thought Foster, and he recalled all those comments his father had written in his journal, the suggestion of cozy intimacy suddenly ringing false—or worse, like the words of a stalker, or of someone used to getting what he wanted.

Jo said, "Yes, so Greg was shocked, but afterwards he was distracted too. We'd talked about getting some lunch the next day, but he didn't show. I figured he'd gone to have it out with Charlie." She paused, long enough to acknowledge Foster's surprise at this admission. "I was right, he did go to confront Charlie, but of course, he was too late."

Foster reached blindly for his wine, took a sip, put the glass back down.

"Gregory Tolman went to the Handeck Glacier? None of the records mention him being there."

"Another of our pointless secrets. When Charlie went missing, we all thought it might complicate things to say Greg had headed up there. Charlie had already set out by the time Greg arrived anyway."

"He arrived that day."

"That's what I said. But he was too late."

"According to who?" Foster struggled to arrange his thoughts, and to put aside his astonishment at Jo's willful avoidance of an obvious truth. "He arrived up there the day my dad disappeared. Was that the day after you and Greg met for drinks?"

"No, it was the day after that."

"The day after that? Maybe . . . thirty-six hours. He claimed he didn't get there until after my dad set out, a claim you were happy to believe, and yet he had an entire day when he was meant to be having lunch with you. He could have been there the night before my dad set out, let alone on the morning itself."

She smiled and shook her head. "Greg slept late the morning after our drink. He set off just before lunch, that's what he told me, and I have no reason to disbelieve him. You also have to remember, Foster, this was over thirty years ago—transport was slower back then."

"No, even if he was telling the truth about sleeping late, he still could have been there earlier than he claimed." She looked unyielding, so he said, "There were indications that Charlie had been in a fight."

She looked suspicious of a trap, saying, "What kind of indications?"

"All you need to know is that the director of the forensic institute told me that anyone who'd been on the mountain that day with my dad would have had some questions to answer."

"Greg wasn't there."

"He could have been."

She sat motionless for a few seconds, then took a deep breath and put her wine aside as if she'd suddenly lost interest in it.

"Maybe," she said finally. "I've thought about it a lot over the years, that year especially. Charlie had disappeared, that was all we knew, and I thought again and again about the timing and how long it might have taken Greg to get there. He wasn't involved in your father's death, Foster, I'm more certain of that than ever, but at the time I worried for him, that he might have done something that could wreck his future, and I worried for Lucy, naturally."

"But not for my father?"

At first it looked like she might not answer, but then she said, "There was a memorial service for him at the university. A lot of people attended. It was so crowded, the five of us couldn't even sit together—Lucy didn't come, as I'm sure you'd understand—and people I didn't even know stood up and expressed overblown platitudes. None of us spoke—we felt we were above such public displays. Ham was very dignified, just as he always is. Giorgio was in floods of tears, and so was Greg. Marianne, just a little. I didn't cry at all. Maybe you'll think I'm a terrible person, but I don't think I ever shed a single tear for Charlie Treherne."

"Wow! So all that stuff about how much you liked him, how much fun he was—"

"Was all true. I *did* like him, and he *was* fun. He was always exciting to be around, but that blinded one to the underlying truth—something I only realized after the incident with Lucy—that he wasn't a good person. Lucy liked Charlie a lot, but never like that, and for Charlie, that was just another challenge. I think he genuinely believed they'd wake up in bed together that next morning, realize this had been waiting to happen for a long time, and become a couple. It's quite a chilling thought, but I think it's who he was."

Foster thought of his dad in that Polaroid, but also of Lisa Kinneston saying it was Charlie who'd covered her with a coat. He was disgusted by the thought of who his father had been, but still wanted something to cling on to, some suggestion that he hadn't been an animal. Then he hit once again on the more fundamental truth.

"Whatever kind of person he was, he didn't deserve what happened to him. Even if it was an accident, if someone played a part in his death, they have to face that, just as he should have faced up to what he did to Lucy."

She looked sympathetic and said, "But he was alone. Giorgio was unwell, Greg didn't arrive until too late."

"Sure, and they both wept bitterly at his memorial." He looked at his wine glass, but he didn't want to drink any more. He could feel a tight knot of anger in his stomach and wasn't even sure what lay behind it. "I want to speak to Gregory Tolman."

"Impossible. I know he won't see you."

"I thought he had nothing to hide." It was a facetious comment, and she didn't respond. Foster knew he'd have the opportunity to see Tolman in due course anyway. So he concentrated his fire on the one other missing link. "But if he won't see me, I want to see Giorgio Pichler, and please don't tell me none of you kept in touch with him."

Far from making that claim again, she said simply, "What do you honestly believe Giorgio can tell you?"

"Clearly something." She looked confused and Foster said, "If the story you're all telling is the truth, Giorgio was probably the last person to see my dad alive, the last person to spend any time in his company. It would have been the most natural thing in the world to facilitate a meeting between me and him. Yet all three of you have claimed to know nothing of his whereabouts or what became of him. I can only conclude that's because you fear he'll tell me something *you* don't want me to hear."

"Ridiculous!" She looked to the house, almost as if wanting to hear the phone ringing now. Then she turned back and said, "We *are* still in touch with him, but Giorgio is very private, removed from the world in many ways. He was deeply upset by Charlie's death. He was unwell that day, but he felt responsible and I think, even now, it would be quite upsetting for him to have to go back over the whole thing."

"I appreciate it wouldn't be easy for him." She nodded, mistakenly thinking Foster had accepted her suggestion of respecting

Giorgio's privacy. "It wasn't easy growing up without parents, either. It's not easy viewing your father's mummified body over thirty years after he died, not easy finding out he might have been a sexual predator and that your very existence might be the result of date rape. So, Gregory Tolman might be out of reach, but one way or another, I intend to speak to Giorgio—I'm just asking you to make it a little easier for me."

She stared at him, her features frozen. Seconds crept past.

"Well, if you put it like that." Still she hesitated, and he increasingly doubted Giorgio Pichler had played any part in his dad's death, but he did wonder if the Italian's testimony would cast doubt on Tolman's story, and that was why they didn't want Foster to meet him. Jo relented and said, "I can give you the address of the Pichlerhof. It's a large farm, high up the side of a valley in the Südtirol. There's no phone number so you can't call. You can write to him or you can visit."

"Then I'll visit."

"As you wish. There's a parking lot, but the final kilometer or so is on foot. It's a celebrated restaurant, open during the day, serving food only from the farm itself, entirely organic. A wonderful place, but you won't be able to fly your private plane into his backyard."

There was something about her tone that suddenly made Foster see what this group would have been like back in its day in Bologna—privileged and dismissive and judgmental all at once. He would have disliked them, he suspected, and certainly wouldn't have wanted to be part of their society.

The New Painters hadn't been quite the same. It had been a much more amorphous grouping of fellow students to begin with, the final dozen only crystallizing in the couple of months before the show. And far from being born of an innate sense of superiority, The New Painters had been designed to help them get a break in the art world against what had seemed like insurmountable odds.

He'd tired of Josefin Widegren now, and wanted only to get Pichler's address and leave. In truth, he'd tired equally of hearing about his father, but he would see this through, whatever this was. In reality, Foster didn't know what Charlie Treherne had deserved, he didn't even know whether he would have liked him had he lived, but Foster still needed to know the truth of what had happened to him.

Twenty-Nine

Josefin Widegren would have been furious, but it proved more straightforward to fly the plane back to Berlin and arrange a new flight to Bolzano late the next morning. He didn't have time to see Daniela, and was relieved in a way, not wanting to tell her that the Polaroid from Yale had not represented some aberration, but was possibly a true indication of who Charlie had been.

Natsuko had arranged a car to meet him at Bolzano, but Jo hadn't been kidding about the location of the Pichlerhof, and the last half-hour of the journey involved a steep climb up the side of the valley on increasingly narrow roads. When they reached the graveled parking lot, where the road gave way to a rough track, they found it almost full with a dozen cars, all high-end marques.

Apart from some wisps of cloud clinging to the distant mountains, the sky was a uniform powder blue, but it was noticeably cooler this high up the side of the valley. Foster set off walking up the track, the ribbons of development and cultivated fields visible on the flat valley floor way below, a much more timeless rustic landscape surrounding him here—neat apple orchards, goats, cows with alpine bells.

It was approaching two o'clock, and before he'd walked far he saw the first of the people heading in the opposite direction, mainly middle-aged couples who looked like early retirees from respectable professions. All but one couple smiled and said hello, all speaking German.

And as he neared the farmstead itself, he could hear the purr of motors starting below and snaking their way slowly back down into the valley. He walked through a yard where chickens wandered freely, and past an open barn which had children's drawings pinned up inside it beyond the farm machinery.

A gate opened onto a terrace where a few people were still eating at hefty wooden tables. There was a restaurant on the far side, with large glass windows looking out over the valley, but Foster could see that it was empty on this sunny spring day. Behind the terrace and raised up a little was the farmhouse itself, more like a grand chalet than something that might once have belonged to peasant farmers.

The sense of peace was mesmerizing. The remaining diners were almost silent, speaking in hushed tones. All was stillness around the buildings of the farmstead. Foster could hear the gentle chorus of cowbells, a tractor some way distant, nothing else.

The door to the restaurant opened and a young man came out carrying a tray with coffees. He nodded at Foster and said something he didn't catch, then walked over to a couple sitting at one of the tables.

Foster didn't respond, momentarily taken aback. It was as if Giorgio Pichler had stepped out of that group photograph and appeared here in front of him. Having delivered the coffees, the man came back over to Foster, speaking warmly as he spun the empty tray in his hand.

"Sorry, I—"

"Ah, American. I was just saying, lunch is nearly finished, but you're welcome to sit, look at the menu, and if we've run out of anything I can tell you."

"Actually, I'm not really hungry."

Giorgio's son—because who else could he be—cocked his head to one side and gave Foster a puzzled smile. "It's a long way to come if you don't want to eat."

"I'm here to see Giorgio Pichler. I'm guessing you're his son?"

"Yeah, Carlo. Can I ask what it's about?"

"Sure. My name's Foster Treherne. Giorgio knew my father. I just wanted to—"

Foster stopped because Carlo Pichler was already nodding. He pointed now to one of the wooden tables.

"Please, take a seat and I'll see if I can find him. You'll at least allow me to bring you some of our cured meats, some cheese, bread?"

"Okay, thanks."

Carlo looked at him for a second, then held out his hand and, as they shook, said, "I'm pleased to meet you, Foster. I was named after your father."

He smiled and walked back into the restaurant, and as Foster sat in the heavy wooden chair he was surprised to find tears in his eyes. In all the people he'd met who'd had some connection with his father, this was the first indication from anyone of any real and deep affection. Giorgio Pichler had named his son after Charlie, which had to count for something.

A short while later, Carlo came back and placed a wooden board in front of Foster, arrayed with cured meats and cheeses. Then he unloaded the tray he carried in his other hand—a basket of bread, a small carafe of red wine, two glasses.

"The wine is from down in the valley. Everything else is from here. Enjoy."

"Thanks."

Carlo crossed the terrace and talked to the remaining customers before walking back into the restaurant. Foster looked at the second glass for a moment or two, then shooed away a fly as it homed in on the folds of ham.

He poured a glass of wine and started to eat, finding his appetite, and was almost finished when a man appeared next to the table. He hadn't emerged from the restaurant and Foster guessed he must have come from the farmhouse itself.

It was Giorgio Pichler, his hair gray but his skin tanned and taut, his frame lean.

"May I join you?"

Father and son even had the same voice, a gentle mournful quality about it.

Foster stood as he swallowed what was in his mouth and put his hand out.

"Herr Pichler, thank you for seeing me."

The older man shook his hand, saying, "Please, call me Giorgio, and why would I not see you? You're always welcome here." Giorgio sat down, smiled to himself as he noticed the extra glass, and poured himself a drink. "Finish your food. It's all from here on the farm."

"It's all good. Did you grow up here?" He continued to eat as Giorgio looked around the terrace with satisfaction.

"No, but I came to stay a lot as a child. The farm belonged to my grandparents. My father had no interest—he had a very successful business of his own—so when my grandfather felt he was getting too old, I took it on and turned it into the Pichlerhof you see today. A passion project. And thankfully, Carlo has inherited the passion."

"He said he was named after my father."

Giorgio nodded, smiling. "I have two sisters, but no brothers. Charlie was like a brother to me. I was so relieved when they found him, but he loved the mountains, he truly did."

Giorgio was the first person to express that sentiment since Professor Dorn had mentioned that people who died in the mountains were dying somewhere they loved.

"I heard you two would go on trips alone, without the others in the Piranesi Society."

Like Marianne Tolman, Giorgio seemed unsurprised by Foster's mention of this supposedly arcane society from their student days.

"Sometimes," he said casually. "We liked the mountains. We both liked to ski. The others did, too, but not so much. We were a good team, Charlie and I."

There was such warmth in Giorgio's face, such benevolent feelings for his long-lost friend and the friend's son sitting in front of him now, that Foster felt bad about asking the questions he had to ask. But he did have to ask them, for his own peace of mind if nothing else.

"Have you heard from any of the others since my dad's body was found? I understand you don't have a telephone here."

He looked bemused. "No telephone? Who told you this? I heard from Chris, and also from Jo."

That explained Giorgio's lack of surprise. And Foster was beginning to understand now why the Piranesi Society had appealed to them so much—they all seemed to have an almost pathological need for secrecy.

"I see, then you'll probably have some idea of the things I want to ask about." Giorgio was still smiling, but didn't respond. "I wanted to ask you first what you thought about what happened between Charlie and Lucy."

Giorgio responded now, pinching his lips together and shaking his head. "To me, it was out of character." The fact he was cutting to the chase suggested Josefin had brought him completely up to speed on how much Foster knew. "He dated a couple of Italian girls I knew and they said he was a complete gentleman. The only time we ever spoke of it, he told me he hadn't behaved as he should have done, but that was it—I didn't want to ask more."

Foster nodded, feeling that was an admission of sorts in itself, that he hadn't wanted to ask because he hadn't wanted to think less of his friend. Foster pushed the wooden board to one side, then refilled both glasses with the red wine.

"Josefin Widegren suggested he might have slipped Lucy a roofie. You know, drugged her drink?"

Giorgio was shaking his head even as Foster spoke.

"Jo, always putting together two and two, and coming up with whichever number she wants. She told you she saw them that night?" Foster nodded and Giorgio said, "Lucy didn't usually drink very much. But Charlie? Charlie could *hold his liquor*, as you Americans say. All that practice at Yale. I don't think I ever saw him drunk. So, if you want to know the truth, I think they went to the party, went back to her room, and the opportunity got the better of him. What he did was wrong, and he knew it, but it wasn't . . . premeditated?" Foster nodded again, acknowledging that he'd chosen the right word. "I would have trusted Charlie Treherne with my life—and I did, several times—and I also believe he knew he'd made a terrible mistake that night."

"You think the others saw it that way?" Giorgio smiled, non-committally, and Foster said, "I'm assuming you and Charlie didn't fight at all, the day before he disappeared?"

"Fight? I never had an argument with Charlie, let alone a fight. I can remember the night before as if it were only yesterday. I was angry with myself because I got so sick with the flu, and we'd planned the next day to hike up to the Handeck Glacier. Charlie told me to relax, said we'd do it together some other time, that I could be more a danger to him if I went along in that condition."

Giorgio shook his head and briefly closed his eyes, probably still thinking he might have saved Charlie if he had been there. And if Foster's instincts were right, that was possibly true.

"Gregory Tolman was there that day, wasn't he?"

"He arrived after lunch."

"You're sure?" Giorgio narrowed his eyes, apparently wanting to know what Foster was getting at. "I know Greg was angry with my dad. He'd spoken to Josefin and she'd told him what she thought had happened. He headed up there to confront Charlie."

"Of course, yes, I know this."

"I viewed my father's body, Giorgio. The buttons were ripped off his shirt, as if he'd been in a scuffle. The skin was even scratched beneath it. It's why I asked if you'd fought with him. You have any other idea how those buttons might have been torn off?"

"Greg didn't arrive until after lunch."

And that was an answer in itself.

"Giorgio, there isn't enough evidence to go to the police about any of this. But I hope you can understand how important it is for me to know. I spent most of my childhood thinking he might still come back. I just want to know why he didn't."

Giorgio nodded and looked over as Carlo came out of the restaurant and headed to one of the tables of remaining diners. Giorgio winked at him and Foster saw Carlo smile back.

"The other people staying at the *pension*, they all left the day before, so Charlie and I were the only people there. There had been talk of snow, and when I woke up that morning I looked out of my window and there was a good covering, and it was still snowing. I thought Charlie might have changed his mind—I even went and knocked on his door. It was the owner's wife who told me he'd gone just after breakfast. We knew he was heading for the Handeck Glacier, but there were several routes and he'd left no word which one he planned to take. I guess he wanted to make the judgment once he was already out there."

"What time was it when you got up?"

"Midmorning, maybe eleven. I felt a lot better. It probably still wouldn't have been wise for me to walk, but I was much improved."

Foster could see the pained calculations still going on deep inside—whether or not he could or should have walked with Charlie that day. Giorgio looked down at the small glass of wine in front of him, moved it idly back and forth across the table like someone might at a séance, and said, "There was a lounge in the *pension* and I was sitting in there reading just after lunch when I heard the front door open. At first I thought it might be Charlie, but it was Greg. When he came into the lounge, the first thing he did was ask me where Charlie was. He seemed agitated. But when I told him Charlie had gone out early he calmed down, apologized, asked how I was. I asked him if everything was okay and he said he needed to speak with Charlie about something, but it could wait."

"Did you have any idea what he wanted to talk to him about?"

"I could guess, naturally. He still seemed angry, but as the afternoon went on, he began to get concerned. It was snowing heavily by now—"

"Did that concern you?"

"Not so much. I knew Charlie's capabilities. But Greg asked me late in the afternoon if Charlie had appeared in a good state of mind. I said he had and asked why. Greg just said Charlie had done a stupid thing, and he was worried he might do something else stupid."

"Suicide?"

"I think that's what he meant. But Charlie wasn't suicidal. Anyway, we didn't raise the alarm until Charlie failed to return by nightfall. It was snowing even more heavily by now. They started to search the next morning, but it was impossible to track him with all the fresh snow. And you know the rest."

"What was Greg like afterward? I mean, how did he behave?"

"He was devastated, more than I would have expected. He and Charlie had been close at the beginning, but by the end they'd drifted apart."

"Are you still in touch with Gregory Tolman?"

"We followed very different paths. We exchange Christmas cards."

"So you've never asked him about what happened that day?"

Giorgio shook his head. "What was there to ask? Everything was so busy for the next few days. And until just the other week, we had no more idea than you did of what happened to Charlie." A small cloud of sadness drifted across his features. "I would have liked to have come to the funeral. I understand why you would wish to keep it for family only, but I hope you know I would have come."

"What family?" Foster felt a sudden flaming of anger. "Who told you I didn't want people there? Josefin?"

"It's not what you wanted?"

"No! I asked both her and Chris Hamblyn if they'd come, and I asked both of them about you. Why were they so afraid of you meeting me? What did they think you'd tell me?"

"I'm sorry, I . . . I would have come, of course I would."

More forcefully now, Foster said, "Giorgio, why didn't they want me to meet you?"

Giorgio stared at him for long seconds, his face so impassive it was impossible to guess at his thought processes, whether he was angry or sad or resolute.

Finally, he said, "Perhaps they were fearful I'd raise questions, questions which have no answers, and what good does it do for you or any of us? But you're Charlie's son. And maybe they were right to be fearful, because I don't think it's correct to withhold the truth from you, even if the truth is only more mystery."

"You think Greg arrived earlier, don't you? You think he was there."

"I don't know." It seemed to pain him that he did not know. "Greg walked up from the village, quite a way in the snow, far enough that it was impossible to know if he'd been walking thirty minutes or three hours. If I have a doubt about his story—and I have carried this doubt all this time—it's about something he said." He finished the wine in his glass, and when Foster picked up the carafe to fill it again, he shook his head and put his hand over the glass. "As I mentioned to you, all the other guests had left the day before, and there had been snowfall. You know that unique acoustic when there's been snow. The inside of the hotel felt hollow, everything echoing. So when Greg came in through the front door, I clearly heard the first words he said. He greeted the owner and said he was looking for Giorgio Pichler."

Foster tried to respond, but found himself unable to, his thoughts racing too quickly. Gregory Tolman had gone to confront Charlie Treherne, had supposedly traveled non-stop from Bologna to get there and walked from the village in heavy snow. Yet his first statement to the owner of the *pension* had been that he was looking for Giorgio, not Charlie. There was only one possible explanation for that.

At last, the obvious question came to him, and Foster said, "Did you ever mention this to anyone? I mean, to the authorities?"

Giorgio shook his head. "It was days later before I thought about it. As I mentioned to you, at that point it didn't seem odd, because I didn't know Charlie was missing. Afterwards, I was caught up in the panic of trying to find him. It was only much later that I thought of it. I mentioned it to Jo and Chris. Jo said I probably remembered wrong. Chris said I was reading too much into it anyway, and that Greg had no reason to lie. Of course, I don't think Chris knew the full story about Charlie and Lucy at that point."

Did anyone know the full story about Charlie and Lucy? Maybe only Charlie, and he was no longer here to tell it.

"And you've never asked Greg about it since?"

"No." He nodded, as if to acknowledge that it was a surprising omission. "I think I was scared to ask him. I liked Greg, and I didn't want to ask him and see in his eyes that he was lying."

"You think he was there?"

"I don't know." But there was no conviction in Giorgio's voice, and he only regained it as he said, "If he was, I think what happened must have been an accident. Greg wasn't violent. None of us were violent people. And if Greg was there and did play a part in what happened to Charlie, I know it would have haunted him, even to this day."

Foster nodded, though he cared little for the haunting or otherwise of Gregory Tolman.

"Thanks for being so honest with me, Giorgio. You're the first of my dad's former friends to do that."

"You're welcome, of course. But what will you do?"

"There isn't much I *can* do. My dad's already in the ground, I'm the last person with any connection to him, and like I said, short of an admission, there isn't enough evidence to interest the police. But I still plan to speak with Greg Tolman."

"He won't talk to you."

"So I keep hearing." Foster finished his wine. "But I'll find a way."

Giorgio nodded, but it was almost as if he were no longer interested in the events of the past, and he said, "I understand you're a very busy man, but it would mean a lot one day if we could welcome you here for a visit. In here . . ." He raised his fist and held it against his heart. "In here, you will always be welcome as a part of my family."

"Thank you."

Foster couldn't say more, ambushed and overwhelmed by how earnest Giorgio was, wishing only that they had met twenty years earlier, that he might have been welcomed into the warm embrace of the Pichlerhof and this family. He could happily have belonged here.

But that just highlighted the true cost of what had happened in the falling snow that day. Whether or not it had been an accident, whether or not Gregory Tolman had been there, the events of that day had ensured that an as-yet-unborn child would never truly belong anywhere.

Thirty

"You're not your father. You're not the good things about him, you're not the bad. You are your own person."

He'd gone to Daniela's apartment in Kreuzberg as soon as he got home, and only now, as they lay in bed in the still of the night, was he talking about the things he'd learned.

Foster said, "I know. It's just tough hearing that kind of stuff. All those childhood fantasies I had where he was some kind of hero who'd had to disappear for mysterious reasons. And now? Quite possibly murdered by a friend who didn't like the fact my dad was a rapist?" He laughed. "No wonder Chris Hamblyn didn't want to give a eulogy."

She laughed too, and they couldn't stop laughing for a little while, finding grim amusement in the situation. But then she pulled herself closer against him and said, "I don't know what he did that night with your mom, and he can't speak for himself, but surely it means something that Giorgio named his son after him."

"I hope so." He'd been staring up at the ceiling, but he turned and kissed her now, then said, "I have to go. I need—"

"To paint, I know." She smiled, and caressed the side of his face, her fingers tracing the contours as if trying to memorize them. "And I have to sleep."

"Okay. Have you ever been to Venice?"

"No."

"Would you like to come? I mean, I'm going to confront the man who might have killed my father, but we could see some of the sights while I'm about it."

She laughed again and said, "Well, when you make it sound so romantic . . ."

"Good. I want you to come."

He kissed her again and then got out of bed and dressed. It was only just after midnight but she was already asleep by the time he left. And he walked back home, through both cities, through the one that was wide awake like him, and the other shut up in sleep and oblivious to the life still going on around it.

Foster wanted to paint, could feel the need as an almost physical sensation, but he didn't head into the studio. He went up to the loft apartment, stood for a second, familiarizing himself once again with its silence and emptiness, then picked up his dad's journal and crashed onto the couch with it.

He started at the final entry and worked his way backward, searching for an entry that might refer to the events of that night— the night of Foster's conception, as it proved to be.

But he quickly realized he'd skipped past it when he spotted a line about Gregory Tolman.

> *G's going to NYC with M. At last! I like him and*
> *all, but he's always there, hovering. It's like having*
> *a chaperone!*

Foster assumed this was when Marianne's father had suffered a heart attack. He moved forward through a couple of pages in which Charlie talked about how quiet it was, and how much work he was getting done, and in which he first mentioned the Handeck Glacier and how it might be a good place for "one of our expeditions."

Then a shiver hit Foster's spine as he saw the words he'd been looking for. And he even remembered seeing them in one of his earlier readings, without appreciating their significance at the time.

Problems for me and L. We shouldn't have gone to that stupid party—it was G's idea anyway and mainly his economics and business friends, too. Not our kind of people at all. I told her I was completely out of it, too, but I'm not sure she believes me. I'll just have to hold my ground on that one. Can imagine how Saint G will react if he finds out. Oops.

It raised so many questions. Foster looked over it as a lawyer might, searching for indications between the words—was he admitting to lying, was he admitting to anything, could anything be inferred? And what of the later crime, if there had been one? How had he thought "Saint G" would react—with anger, with violence even?

But above all, Foster kept coming back to that final word— "Oops." Was he reading too much into it? It was a casual throwaway in a private journal, possibly a bit of careless bravado behind closed doors, masking a genuine remorse at what he'd done. That was how Foster wanted to read it, but he couldn't. He looked at that one small word, and all he could see was the arrogant swagger of the young man in the Polaroid.

He went through the remaining pages again, but there was no more mention of it. There was no more mention of L either, not until the final entry where Charlie noted that she'd gone back to England. Foster had no way of knowing what their relationship had been like in the weeks after, whether they'd gone back to being friends, more or less as they had been before, or whether awkwardness and suspicion had driven them apart.

Foster put the book aside. He didn't want to paint now. He felt too tired, a fatigue like none he'd known before, so profound that he couldn't even lift himself from the couch, and in the end he simply lay where he was and didn't wake until midmorning.

When he got down to the office, he found Natsuko and Maja—Axel had a day off.

Natsuko talked him through the plans for Venice and Foster said, "I've asked Daniela to come—will that be a problem?"

"Not at all. The only possible issue would be an extra invite for the party at the Guggenheim, but if necessary, she can just go instead of me."

"But you're still coming to Venice?"

"Sure. And I'll try for an extra invite—they're so thrilled you've decided to come, I'm sure they'll give us one—but it's a fallback position if we need it."

Hearing that the organizers were thrilled by his agreement to attend filled Foster with unease. It was one of the reasons he didn't go along to these kinds of events anymore. He just couldn't stand the fawning and all the people talking with great passion and expertise on a subject no one really understood. Why was one artist more successful than another? Why was Foster a superstar in the art world while Polly Carmichael had been reduced to sending threatening notes?

With that thought, he glanced at Natsuko's desk, but he couldn't see any Comic Sans letters, and he was distracted then as Maja said, "Oh, Foster, here's the preliminary report we put together on that guy Gregory Tolman." She held up a few sheets of paper. "Nothing too exciting. Want me to summarize?"

"If you could." He took the file from her anyway.

Maja said, "Okay, estimated worth of eleven billion, most of it from his company, Tolman Stone. Married Marianne Arthur in 1992. They had three children, divorced in 2005. Married for the second time in 2010, Sarah Denton, no children. A Democrat, but very much on the right of the party. There's increasing speculation that he's mobilizing for a run at Mayor of New York City. He supports a lot of art-based charities—it was his first wife's passion, apparently, but he's kept up with it."

"His first wife has an amazing art collection in her apartment, and a lot more in storage, including a couple of mine."

Natsuko said, "It must run in the family. Her grandparents championed Picasso and Braque and a whole handful more."

Foster thought of the apartment and said, "Doesn't surprise me somehow."

He turned back to Maja, but she shrugged, saying, "That's about it, really, apart from all the minor details. His life isn't that interesting. We're still waiting for the corporate intelligence report from Hamer."

"Is that the former Kroll guy?"

"Yeah. I doubt it'll turn up anything scandalous. He seems completely above board."

"Do we know where he'll be staying in Venice?"

Maja looked at Natsuko, exchanging a smile that suggested they'd discussed this at length. "I guess this is what you do when you're Gregory Tolman—he'll be staying on his own yacht."

"Of course."

Foster remembered his first time in Venice for the Biennale, seeing two or three superyachts moored between the Danieli and the Arsenale and wondering who owned boats like that. He guessed he knew the answer now—people like Gregory Tolman.

Thirty-One

Daniela had never been to Venice, so Foster had the launch take them the long way around from the airport so that they could enter the Grand Canal at the south end, passing Piazza San Marco on the way. She was mesmerized by the whole spectacle, and so was Natsuko, even though she'd been there a handful of times before.

Foster was curious to see if there were any large yachts moored along the stretch from San Marco to the Arsenale, and was disappointed when he found none there. Maybe Tolman's boat was moored elsewhere in the city, or maybe he hadn't arrived yet—the party wasn't until the next night.

They passed Santa Maria della Salute and headed into the Grand Canal, threading between vaporettos and gondolas and water taxis.

Natsuko pointed for Daniela's sake and said, "That's where the party is tomorrow."

"On that little terrace?"

"No, the sculpture garden's inside, much bigger. There'll be a couple of hundred people there."

Foster looked across as the Guggenheim slipped behind them, but his heart sank a little at the thought of the party and those couple of hundred people. Still, he had to focus on just one of them.

They reached the Ca' Sagredo, but checked in and then almost immediately left again. Natsuko went off to spend the next day and a half at the Biennale, while Foster and Daniela spent the same time drifting around the city, not touching any of the obvious sites, but losing themselves instead among the narrow streets.

On the hotel's rooftop terrace the next evening, they drank long drinks and watched the sun sinking over the city, and Natsuko gave them a rundown of the Biennale. There was more figurative painting this time, she thought, and the really interesting conceptual pieces all seemed to be from Asia.

Daniela said, "Oh, but we saw some wonderful pieces from the Caribbean this morning—Grenada and the Dominican Republic; Guatemala, too."

Natsuko looked wide-eyed, as if to ask how she'd missed that, and Foster said, "Not at the main sites. They're all in a little palazzo not far from here—we just stumbled across it."

In fact, it was the only art they'd seen in the city.

Natsuko nodded with determination and said, "Okay, I have to do that tomorrow."

"Who's in the US pavilion this year?"

"Steiner & Badham video installations. They were okay, I guess."

Steiner & Badham was actually just one person, Joe Badham, a guy who filmed things like dripping paint in super-slow motion and replayed them with a synthesized soundscape. Foster had seen a few of them and found them occasionally beautiful and calming, but also completely meaningless. Joe himself talked about his work as if he'd split the atom.

"Will he be at the party?"

"I believe so." As if sensing Foster's enthusiasm ebbing even more, she said quickly, "But you know who else is gonna be there? Theaster Gates."

"Oh good, I like Theaster."

Daniela smiled and said, "I *love* Theaster Gates. I mean his art, obviously—I've never met him, but I'd like to."

Foster smiled, remembering that it was her interest in art that had made her volunteer to chaperone him through the business of reclaiming his father. That had been Foster's lucky break. She looked beautiful tonight, wearing a black cocktail dress and white sneakers, and with her short hair finishing off the look, he was pretty sure most of the pseuds at this party would gravitate toward her, thinking she had to be a powerful player in the art world rather than a diplomat.

Natsuko looked over the Murano glass flowers on the railing to the Grand Canal far below and said, "Our launch is here."

"Then we should go, I guess."

He signed for the drinks and they made their way down and headed back along the canal in the launch. Once they reached the Guggenheim, they turned off into one of the smaller canals and briefly got caught up in a traffic jam of launches and water taxis as other guests arrived.

And when they approached the gate in the wall, Foster could already hear the hubbub inside. He had to fight the urge to turn around and head right back to the boat.

"Foster!" A woman with a mass of red hair and a chalk-white complexion walked toward him, her face beaming yet oddly frozen. "How wonderful to see you, darling! It's been far too long."

"Well, you know me, I don't like attending too many of these things."

Despite her striking appearance he had absolutely no idea who she was, but Natsuko stepped forward and said, "Hey Joan, you probably don't remember me—Natsuko—but it's great to see you again. And may I introduce you to Daniela, Foster's girlfriend."

"Oh, how charming!"

As "Joan" air-kissed Daniela, Foster smiled to himself, somehow touched by the notion that Daniela was his girlfriend—it had a suggestion of permanence about it, even though he was careful not to believe in permanence.

Then he heard Natsuko say, "We must catch up with you later, Joan. See you inside."

"Of course, darling, yes, so much to catch up on."

That was one of the many reasons Foster liked having Natsuko with him at this kind of thing. She shepherded them inside now, through the courtyard where people were milling about, up the steps, and beyond the second tier of security into the sculpture garden itself.

He scanned the crowd, but there were too many people, and with twilight setting in, the lanterns spaced around the sculpture garden didn't do enough to illuminate the faces. They took drinks as they were proffered them and entered the throng.

Almost immediately, a man of about his own age wearing a pale-cream suit approached and introduced himself as Edgar Moreton from the Bureau of Educational and Cultural Affairs, saying how thrilled he was that "the great Foster Treherne" had agreed to attend. The English part of Foster's makeup suspected sarcasm, but the sentiment was probably genuine.

Shelley Kim came over to him then—an abstract painter he'd known pretty well in his New York days. They chatted for a couple of minutes, and by the time he left her, he saw that he'd lost both Daniela and Natsuko and felt suddenly adrift.

He spotted Theaster Gates over by the stone gazebo on the far side and they waved to each other, but as Foster started to head over there he was intercepted again and again, mostly by people who were vaguely familiar but whose names he couldn't remember.

Briefly, he thought he saw someone who looked like Gregory Tolman, but lost him again almost immediately. And then he got trapped in a conversation with two writers, one a freelancer, the other an editor at *New Art Periodical*—the latter kept referencing events where he and Foster had been together in New York, events Foster couldn't even recall.

He escaped them when he heard a public-address system kicking into life. He'd never met anyone who liked the speeches at parties, but he made his excuses and weaved his way among the partygoers and through the gap in the hedge to the other part of the garden, by the café.

Here, on the steps, Edgar Moreton was standing with a microphone, and as soon as he felt he had as much attention as he was likely to get, he started to talk about the long tradition of American artists in Venice.

But Foster was only half-listening, his attention focused instead on the man standing to Edgar Moreton's right in a smart dark suit, himself overlooked by someone who was clearly a bodyguard. The man in the dark suit was Gregory Tolman, and at this distance, in the forgiving light of the sculpture garden, he looked completely unchanged from the young man in the group photo of the Piranesi Society.

Edgar gestured to someone in the crowd below him and said, "It's a great pleasure to have with us this evening this year's artist-in-residence at the American pavilion, *Steiner & Badham!*" A polite round of applause sounded, not matching the enthusiasm of Edgar's announcement, though that was probably the result of people trying to clap while holding flutes of prosecco. "And we're equally lucky to have with us some of the illustrious alumni of biennales past, Foster Treherne, Mark Bradford . . ."

Foster stopped listening altogether. At the mention of his own name, a few people standing nearby turned and smiled at him, but more importantly, Gregory Tolman reacted with barely concealed alarm. He scanned the crowd immediately below where he stood on the steps, then spoke to his bodyguard who, in turn, appeared to speak to someone remotely.

There was another round of applause, and then Edgar said, "And I'd also like to welcome one of the great modern patrons of the arts, and ask him to say just a few words. Please give a warm welcome to Mr. Gregory Tolman."

Greg took the microphone and immediately seemed to have put aside any alarm he'd experienced at the mention of Foster's name.

"Thanks, Edgar." He looked out at the crowd, every inch the politician rather than the businessman. "It's a great honor to be here among so much extraordinary artistic talent. And you know, it's fitting that we're in the former home of Peggy Guggenheim. Because America has always championed the arts, and in these politically divisive times, I truly believe it's our *art* that has the ability to unite and bring people together . . ."

Behind Foster, someone said, "Jeez, you'd think the guy was running for Mayor of New York City," and a few people laughed.

And by the time Foster tuned back in, Gregory Tolman had wound up and was handing back the microphone, much to the apparent surprise of Edgar Moreton, who'd possibly expected a more substantial speech.

"Thanks, Mr. Tolman, and thank you for being here to help celebrate with us this evening. And so it just remains for me to say—please, everyone, enjoy, and have a wonderful evening."

The weak but sustained applause started again and Foster began to push forward as Edgar, Gregory Tolman, and finally the bodyguard descended into the crowd. But everyone was moving now and almost immediately an elderly bearded man took Foster's hand and shook it vigorously.

"Mr. Treherne! You won't remember me—of course not, why would you—but I've followed your career this last decade with such satisfaction."

"Thank you, I—"

"Yes, I know, and that's quite all right. You know, I was one of the first people in New York to buy your work, before you'd even moved to the city."

"Well, I appreciate that, thank you. If you'd just excuse me for a moment, I have to try to catch Gregory Tolman."

"Of course, my dear boy, of course. In fact it was his . . . now let me think . . . his *first* wife who introduced me to your work."

"Marianne Tolman? Yes, I knew she had a couple of mine."

"Oh, at least, but I won't keep you." He was still gripping Foster's hand. "It really has been a pleasure."

He finally let go and Foster said, "Thanks, I appreciate it."

Foster pushed on, but there was no sign of Tolman now. He spotted Natsuko in conversation with Joan, the red-haired woman they'd seen earlier, but he couldn't see Daniela anywhere, either.

He kept looking, but it was another five minutes before he spotted Edgar Moreton. He was talking to Joe Badham of Steiner & Badham, but Foster walked up to him anyway.

"Sorry to interrupt, Edgar. I was hoping to catch Gregory Tolman."

Edgar said, "Too late, sorry. I had hoped he'd hang out for a little while longer, but I guess he has some urgent business to take care of. You know how it is with these people."

"Of course. Not to worry."

Foster was actually thinking that he needed to find Natsuko and work on a backup plan. He hadn't come to Venice and this party only to fail in the main objective of seeing Gregory Tolman.

Joe Badham turned to him now and said, "It's Foster Treherne, isn't it?"

Joe was in his forties, dressed like a Beat poet, and with a graying soul patch that looked like an unfortunate skin complaint beneath his lower lip. They'd met a few times and Foster had no doubt Joe knew exactly who he was—it was a weird power play by an artist who'd felt overlooked for too long and now believed he'd hit the big time.

"It is. Congratulations. I'm hearing great things about the pavilion."

"Thanks. It's nice to be able to fully test the limits of the space, you know, push at the boundaries of what art can do."

"Excellent. Well, if you'll excuse me. Thanks again for the party, Edgar."

"You're more than welcome, and it truly was an honor."

Foster left them and threaded back through the crowd, into the main part of the garden. But he could no longer see anyone, not Natsuko, not Shelley Kim or Theaster Gates, not even the old guy who'd been one of his earliest collectors.

And then, unexpectedly, an avenue seemed to open through the crowd, and there at the end of it was Daniela, smiling at him. He raised his almost empty glass, and she raised hers in return, and he tried to put aside his fear that this could not last, and only thought how lucky he was to have her now.

He walked to meet her, kissed her, held her briefly, and said, "Wow, I've missed you."

"Me too. It's been at least twenty minutes."

"Are you done? Can we get out of here?" He looked around. "I mean, I don't mind if you want to meet some more people. Gregory Tolman left and I didn't get to meet him, so . . . I guess I'll have to go knock on his door, or whatever the superyacht equivalent is."

She nodded. "I would've liked to have met Theaster Gates, but I'm ready. Do we know where Natsuko is?"

"I'll message her. She might want to stay." Daniela was smiling at him in a way he didn't understand, and in the end, Foster said, "What?"

"Nothing. Just . . . I think you'll hear from Gregory Tolman. I zeroed in on his head of security, let him know where you're staying, stressed how beneficial it would be for his boss to meet you here in Venice rather than subsequently."

"You think it'll work?"

"I think he'll get the message." She poured some of her prosecco into Foster's glass. "If Tolman's serious about hitting the campaign trail, he won't want you causing problems down the line."

She raised her glass now and he followed suit, confident she was right, but for the moment not being able to see past her beauty and how much he wanted her in his life. He drank, then reached for his phone and sent a message to Natsuko. One way or another, he wanted out of here.

Thirty-Two

Natsuko stayed on at the party. Foster and Daniela went back to the hotel and ate in the restaurant, on the veranda overlooking the Grand Canal. Foster sent the launch back for Natsuko, but she hadn't returned by the time they went up to bed.

When he woke the next morning, he was alone. He assumed Daniela must have gone for breakfast, but then saw it was already approaching eleven. It wasn't until he'd showered and dressed that he saw the note on the bedside table.

It was handwritten on headed notepaper.

> *Dear Foster, I was sorry to miss you last night at the party. Had I known in advance that you would be there, I would have made it a priority to meet with you. Maybe we could remedy that today. I've booked a table for lunch, 1.30 at the Locanda Cipriani, and would be delighted if you could make it. If you can't, or have other commitments, please do call on the above number and we can try to arrange something else that works for both of us. Otherwise, I look forward to seeing you later today.*

With kind regards,
Greg Tolman

Foster smiled with satisfaction, not on his own account but because of the easy skill with which Daniela had engineered this meeting. All of Greg's former friends in the Piranesi Society had assured Foster he wouldn't agree to see him, yet Daniela had changed the great man's mind in one brief conversation with his head of security.

He found the note interesting in itself, too. Greg couldn't resist phrasing the invitation as if the meeting had been entirely his idea. At the same time, he didn't engage in even the pretense of needing to introduce himself—he knew full well that Foster knew who he was, and he'd probably been updated by Josefin and the others on Foster's reasons for wanting to see him.

Foster checked the time, then made his way to Natsuko's room. He didn't want to disturb her if she'd had a late night, but even as he reached the door he could hear her talking, then Daniela's voice. He knocked and, a moment later, Natsuko came and opened the door, looking remarkably fresh-faced.

"Hey Foster, come on in."

"Thanks. What time did you get back?"

She shrugged. "About midnight. We went to some terrible sports bar near the Rialto. But I'm getting much too old for this."

He laughed. She was twenty-five.

As he walked in he saw Daniela, hunched over a laptop at the ornate desk, scribbling notes on a pad to one side. She saw him and smiled.

"Hey. You got the note?"

He nodded and walked over and kissed her before saying, "Good job. You wanna come?"

"To lunch?"

"Yeah, it's a great place, out on Torcello."

She smiled, baffled, and said, "Another time, maybe. I think this is something you really need to do on your own. He might talk to you, but he'll clam up if there's someone else there." She pointed at the laptop. "That said, we've got something pretty strange here, something that maybe changes a few things."

Natsuko said, "It's definitely pretty strange." She looked at Foster. "We got the report back from Hamer. Most of it's not at all interesting, but he spotted an anomaly with some shell companies owned by Tolman Stone and started digging and cross-referencing. I'm not sure you're gonna like what he found."

"Okay." He sat on the edge of the bed. Daniela turned to face him.

Natsuko perched on the armchair, then said, "Gregory Tolman has never bought one of your works."

"His first wife bought two."

Natsuko corrected him. "In fact, his first wife has bought a total of six over the years."

Foster was surprised, but remembered the old guy from the party. When Foster had mentioned that Marianne owned two of his paintings, the old guy had said "at least." Foster hadn't taken in what he meant by that at the time, but it made sense now.

"Now, even with the forensic work Hamer does, there's a limit to what he can find out, but of all your paintings that sold in the original New Painters exhibition, at least five were bought either by people with strong associations with Gregory Tolman, or in two cases, by shell companies owned by Tolman Stone."

Foster seemed to hear the words and not hear them, to be there and not, reality shifting fleetingly around him, as if he could briefly sense a fissure in his existence that he hadn't been aware of before. It was as if Natsuko had picked up that laptop and smacked him over the head with it.

If what she was telling him was true, he had never been the breakout success of The New Painters, had never struck that fabled vein of immediate success. Instead, the man who'd quite possibly played a part in his father's death had gamed the market in his favor.

"That's why I sold and the others didn't."

Daniela offered a sympathetic smile and said, "There's more."

Natsuko nodded. "Over the next two to three years, it's hard to be exact, but in both the shows and the resale market, there are a lot of sales linking back to Tolman in the same way. You remember when one of your *Brueghel* series was in the Contemporary American auction at Sotheby's New York?"

"Of course." As if it could possibly have slipped his mind—the first time a painting of his had come up at auction, selling way above estimate and setting the record for the entire sale. But he also knew what was coming.

"The winning bid was from a trust belonging to Marianne Tolman. The vendor—a shell company owned by Tolman Stone."

You're a fraud. That's what those notes from Polly or her husband had kept saying, and as it turned out, they were right. He wasn't fraudulent himself, nor was his art, but his success was nothing more than a scam, carried out on Foster as much as it had been on the art world.

Foster looked at the two of them and said, "He manipulated the market. People buy what's already selling. Then more people buy, and then because people keep seeing my paintings, they become familiar and things develop a momentum of their own. That's why I was a success and the others weren't. It's the only reason."

Natsuko was shaking her head, but to his surprise Daniela said, "You might be right. You know how much I love art, but really, isn't the whole market a kind of . . . illusion? Doesn't it all just rely on showing people something enough times that it becomes familiar to them? I guarantee half the people who first saw a Basquiat thought some little kid had done it. I've seen your loft, Foster, and some of those other painters were talented and they should've made it, and if it hadn't been for Gregory Tolman, maybe you wouldn't have made it either, but that doesn't mean you don't deserve what you have."

Natsuko said, "Daniela's right. So you slept with a Medici. It doesn't stop you being Michelangelo."

Foster laughed, then Daniela and Natsuko did too, and he knew they were both right. Besides, he'd felt like an impostor his whole career, like someone who didn't really belong at the top table—once he'd gotten over the shock, he felt this confirmation of that belief could even be liberating.

It had always been about the painting for him. He'd never cared for the fame or the art world or all the other things that came with it. As much as he valued the freedom of success, the benefits of being able to buy spacious studios and hire support staff, it always came back to the paint, and this news could never change that.

But then, as Daniela's smile fell away again, she said, "The only question is, why did he do it? I mean, from what you've told me—say Giorgio Pichler had been the billionaire, I could easily imagine him buying your paintings. I mean, he named his son after your dad, so that would make sense. But Greg and Charlie . . . I'm trying to think of some other reason, but for me it's all pointing one way."

Natsuko nodded somberly, and in the end so did Foster. There were probably many reasons why someone might go to great lengths to anonymously support the child of a long-dead friend. And Daniela was right—if it had been Giorgio Pichler behind his career, the explanation would most likely have been benign.

But Greg and Charlie had not been friends, certainly not at the end. And the Piranesi had gone to great lengths to conceal and protect him, and had been insistent from the start that he wouldn't want to meet Foster. Why would people behave like that, and why would Tolman go to such lengths, unless it was to appease his guilt?

Thirty-Three

He took the launch, heading across the lagoon to Torcello, the breeze deceptively fresh. As soon as the driver slowed and entered the canal on the far side of the island, the heat settled back over them.

He stepped onto the landing near the Locanda, earning curious glances from the handful of tourists who'd come in on the vaporetto and were wandering around listlessly in the early-afternoon sun, almost as if stunned by the relative peace they'd found here after being in the city.

Foster passed through the dark interior of the restaurant and out into the rear courtyard, where nearly every table was full, waiters in white tunics gliding seamlessly among them. One of the waiters turned as Foster stepped out, looking ready to tell him they had no more space.

But then he smiled with recognition and said, "Ah, Signor Treherne, welcome back!"

Some of the diners nearby turned to look at this new arrival who was perhaps famous enough or a regular enough visitor to be recognized.

"Thanks, it's good to be back."

"Your guest has already arrived. We have a table set up in the garden. Let me show you."

Foster looked across the gravel courtyard, and over the low hedge to the garden beyond. Some twenty feet from the nearest fellow diners, a table had been set up under the shade of an umbrella, and Gregory Tolman was sitting there with the same bodyguard from the previous night.

Foster glanced around, assuming there would be more than one person in Greg's security team, even here, then turned to the waiter and said, "It's okay, I can see it—I'll find my own way."

"As you wish. I'll be over soon to take your order."

Foster walked between the tables and out onto the lawned path through the ornamental gardens beyond. As he approached, the bodyguard stood and left, nodding respectfully to Foster as their paths crossed.

Greg Tolman stood too, and came around the table, a broad smile and his hand outstretched as he said, "Foster, I'm so glad you could make it. Thanks for coming."

"Thanks for inviting me." He shook Greg's hand, parchment-dry despite the heat. His hair was dyed, which was one of the reasons he looked so youthful and unchanged from a distance, but close up it had the opposite effect, highlighting the fact that his skin had lost all its youthful elasticity—Greg looked after himself, clearly, but there was something of a waxwork quality about him. Foster added, "I was told you might not want to meet with me."

The smile barely faltered, and as he gestured for Foster to sit, he said, "I can guess who by. She means well, but too protective."

Foster wasn't sure if he meant Josefin or Marianne, but Giorgio had also expressed a doubt about Greg Tolman's willingness to see him. Greg looked around then.

"Isn't this place magnificent? It's over thirty years since I last came to this restaurant. Honestly, that's why I chose it for our meeting." Foster didn't respond. He sensed Greg was trying to set up a story, and Foster felt disinclined to play his part. Sure enough, after the pause that Foster had been meant to fill with a question, Greg nodded and said, "Charlie and I both arrived in Italy at the same time, on the same flight, in fact. Neither of us had been to Venice before so we visited for a few days in our first weeks, late September, when we were still finding our feet. We came here for lunch one day. Charlie's idea, of course—because of Hemingway—but we loved the place. We kept saying we'd come back, never did. In fact, surprisingly, the Piranesi never came to Venice at all."

"I hadn't realized you and my father were such good friends."

Foster knew from the journal that they had been at first, but he was testing the waters and Greg Tolman looked stung as he said, "No, not in the end, we weren't. But early on there was a real bond between us. I was sad that we grew apart the way we did."

He looked over Foster's shoulder and picked up the menu in response. Foster assumed he'd spotted the waiter heading toward them, but he left his own menu on the table.

When the waiter arrived, Foster looked at him and smiled, saying, "I think I'll have the carpaccio followed by the tagliolini, some sparkling mineral water, and maybe a glass of Ripasso." The waiter's name suddenly came back to him, and he added, "Thanks, Andrea."

"Always a pleasure, Signor Treherne."

Andrea turned to Greg, who closed his menu and said, "I'll have the same, but maybe we could get a bottle of the Ripasso instead of two glasses."

"Of course." The waiter took the two menus and left.

"So I assume you're something of a regular here."

"I come whenever I'm in the city, usually about once a year. Do you mind if I call you Greg?"

"Not at all."

"Good. So I'm guessing you know why I wanted to see you, Greg? You mentioned the Piranesi in passing without feeling the need to explain it, even though you've publicly erased any record of you being part of that society. So Chris Hamblyn and Josefin Widegren, and maybe even Marianne, have no doubt kept you up to date on my inquiries."

Greg smiled, but it was strained, and he said, "I understood you were trying to find out a little more about your father and his friends, and how he came to be where he was when he died. I can imagine these recent weeks must have been very difficult for you, not that you imagined he would ever return, but even so."

In his own mind, Foster corrected Greg Tolman, but he didn't say it aloud, somehow feeling that this former friend didn't deserve to hear the truth, that Foster *had* imagined his father returning, that a small vestige of the child he'd once been had kept imagining it right up until the discovery of the body.

Another glance from Greg was enough to let Foster know the waiter was heading in their direction, and they lapsed into silence while water was poured and the wine was opened and tasted. Then, almost immediately, two more waiters came with bread and the starters.

For a few minutes afterwards, they ate in near silence, and Foster relished the peace—only the gentle chatter and clatter of the diners behind him, the soft engine-moan of a jet descending to the airport in the distance beyond Greg Tolman's shoulder.

Foster took a sip of his wine, but no more than that, conscious that the beef and bread were the first things he'd eaten today, then said, "I'm surprised. If you thought I was just trying to find out about my father and his friends, why all the secrecy? You went to so much trouble to avoid me, even getting a picture photoshopped, yet in the end, you agreed to meet me quite easily."

Greg looked momentarily uncomfortable before saying, "Yes, on reflection it might have been better to meet with you in the first place. The Piranesi was the subject of all manner of absurd rumors at Bologna. It's the kind of thing that can raise questions about someone with political ambitions. Were you to release the original photograph, I think my decision about whether to run for office would be made for me."

He fell silent as the waiter arrived to clear the plates. But the impression he'd given was that the secrecy had all been about covering up his involvement with the Piranesi, to stop it endangering his chances of a political career. Hadn't Daniela suggested as much? And maybe that was part of it, but Foster was still convinced it wasn't *all* of it.

Once they were alone again, Foster said, "I have no interest in the Piranesi Society or in publishing that picture. I wanted to meet you because you were there that day, the day Charlie disappeared."

Greg didn't seem surprised by the change of focus. "Yes, I was there. I arrived just after lunch."

"Because you wanted to confront him. Jo Widegren told you what everyone suspected, that he'd had sex with Lucy while—at the very least—she was too drunk to give consent or otherwise." Greg looked pained by the indelicate reminder of what had lain behind his mad dash to Switzerland all those years ago. Foster continued, "You were angry and you wanted to confront him and ask him to his face if he could deny it was true."

"I *was* angry. The whole group of us were so close, had done so many amazing things together. We trusted each other. And if this was true, it was a betrayal of that trust. I think we held ourselves to a higher code in the Piranesi, and Charlie broke that code by doing what he did."

"So there was no question in your mind that he was guilty?"

"No." Despite the certainty, Greg's face appeared to soften a touch as he said, "I didn't want to believe it. I knew he had his reckless side, but this was different. Unlike the others, I also knew he'd been in the Wig & Pen at Yale, but that seemed so out of character for the person I knew. I was confident it had just been a stupid phase, that he'd left it all behind."

"You couldn't have been that confident." In response to Greg's questioning look, Foster added, "You don't tear across northern Italy to confront someone you think is being unfairly maligned."

"Ah. Well, I also had my impetuous side, but no, I guess on balance I found it all too plausible. There was a side to Charlie that was . . . untamed."

"So I keep hearing. Frankly, I'm amazed any of you stayed friends with him."

"That isn't fair."

"On him or on you?"

Greg ignored the question, saying, "I thought if I looked him in the eye, I'd know if it was true." He sighed. "But alas, I was too late."

Foster stared at him for a second or two, taking in the unshakable demeanor that would serve him well in a political career, then said, "No, I don't think you were too late, Greg. I think you're lying."

"Excuse me?" He sounded hostile, even threatening. "You need to be very careful what you're saying, young man." And in that response, in the patronizing address, Foster was convinced he'd seen the truth. "Don't accuse someone of lying unless you have . . ." He left the admonition hanging and broke into a slick smile for the approaching waiters, and chatted amiably about the gardens and the food as the mains were laid out before them.

When the waiters left, Greg looked disinclined to eat, but Foster was hungry and started on his pasta. Reluctantly, it seemed, Greg started to eat too, but put his fork down again after just a few mouthfuls.

"What are you basing this accusation on, Foster?"

Foster finished what he was eating and said, "Couple of different things. Not least the fact that *someone* was on the mountain with my dad, and it wasn't Giorgio. And is it such a wild accusation? Even Josefin told me she'd wondered over the years whether you might have been involved." Greg leaned back in his chair, contemplating him, but Foster said, "You'll have to excuse me, but this is breakfast for me."

He went back to his pasta and Greg watched him in silence for a while, before saying, "It's not a wild accusation, I'll grant you that. And that's why I have to be so vigorous in defending myself against it. These kinds of rumors have a way of developing their own momentum."

"Much like the rumors about what happened between two people late at night after a party."

"No, not like that at all." There was absolute certainty in Greg's voice, but he sat without speaking for another little while, before saying, "Why are you so convinced someone was on the mountain with him?"

Foster paused from eating now and said, "There's something I need to say first. I won't be going public with this. There isn't enough evidence for the police to be involved and I don't want this kind of publicity, not for me, not for my father. If I'm right, I want you to tell me the truth, that's all. From what I've heard so far, I'm guessing even the other members of the Piranesi don't know what really happened, although they might have guessed and have been happy to rally around you anyway, so it's possible you've never told anyone what actually happened that day. Well, this is your chance. If I'm right, I want you to tell me. I'm Foster Treherne, and I think that gives me some right to hear the truth."

"You still haven't answered my question."

"Okay." Foster picked up the bottle of wine and poured more into both glasses before leaning back in his chair. "Firstly, three buttons were torn from my dad's shirt. The director of the forensic institute said it looked like he'd been in a scuffle. His view was that it still didn't provide evidence of a crime, but that if someone else had been on the mountain that day, that person would have some questions to answer." He allowed Greg the opportunity to say something, but he remained silent, so Foster continued. "So, it seems likely someone was up there. Why do I think it was you? You traveled all the way from Bologna to Switzerland to confront my dad, you arrived at the *pension* just after lunch, you walked in, saw the owner, and what did you say? Not, 'I'm looking for Charlie Treherne.' You walked in and said, 'I'm looking for Giorgio Pichler.' Why? Because you already knew Charlie wasn't there. You walked into the lounge and asked Giorgio where Charlie was, but the question he'd heard you ask the owner—that was the giveaway. You knew Charlie wasn't there because you'd been on the mountain with him." Greg Tolman continued to stare, his thoughts so hard to read that, in the end, Foster said, "Well? Am I right?"

Still he sat in silence, and seconds crept past and another plane descended into the airport, and finally he said, "I always wondered if Giorgio had overheard me. I never asked him about it. Good of him to keep it quiet all this time, of course, particularly given how close the two of them were."

"So you *were* there, on the mountain?"

Foster could see a dramatic shift in Greg's countenance. It was as if he were physically shedding some burden he'd carried all this time.

"Yes." Greg appeared to weigh up if that simple answer was enough. "Yes. I was there."

"And will you tell me what happened?"

Greg Tolman lowered his eyes, looking not at Foster now but at the glass of wine in front of him, apparently deep in thought, until finally, as if to himself, he nodded.

Thirty-Four

"I don't think I've ever been as angry as I was when Jo told me about Charlie and Lucy. I knew they'd slept together, and even that was . . . Well, when Jo told me that Charlie might have slipped her a roofie, I was furious."

"Giorgio didn't believe the story about the roofie. He just thought Charlie could handle a drink and Lucy couldn't."

Grudgingly, Greg Tolman said, "Yeah, I think that's true. I didn't at the time." He frowned. "The night Jo told me, I even looked to see if I could take a sleeper train up to Switzerland. In the end, I didn't sleep at all and I left the next morning, stayed in some small hotel near the station in Brig—I don't even remember the name of it or anything about it. I left at six the morning after that. There was already snow on the ground, but it had started snowing again when I arrived, and then as I was walking up from the village I saw someone leave the *pension* and head off onto one of the trails. I knew right away it was Charlie. He had this bright-red hiking jacket."

"I know, I've seen it, in the mortuary."

"Of course." There was a flash of sympathy in his eyes—for Foster, presumably, rather than for Charlie.

"Did you try to call after him?"

Greg shook his head. "He was too far off. I wondered why Giorgio wasn't with him, but I thought that might provide an ideal opportunity. So I just set off after him, but Charlie . . . he and Giorgio were naturals in the mountains. It took me every effort even to keep him in sight. I might not have caught up with him at all, but after an hour or so he reached a point overlooking the edge of the glacier and stopped to look. He turned, saw me. I don't know if he even knew it was me at that stage—he waited anyway. It was still snowing a little, but I remember, as I got closer, Charlie unzipped his jacket."

"Why do you think he did that?"

"Probably just hot. It wasn't all that cold, even up there and in the snow, and it was a tough climb."

"You said not having Giorgio around might provide an ideal opportunity. For what?"

"We'd grown apart, the two of us, but despite everything we were still close, we still had that bond we'd made early on. I thought if it was just him and me, he'd be more open."

"And?"

Greg laughed ruefully, the air of a man who'd replayed the events of that day countless times in the years since, probably imagining how it might have ended differently. He finished his wine and Foster shared the remains of the bottle between their two glasses.

"Thanks." He picked up his glass and took another sip before continuing. "If anything, he was too open, certainly too open for my liking. He denied spiking her drink and gave the same version that Giorgio imagined, up to a point. He admitted that she was . . . if not unconscious, at least completely unaware of what was going on. *You don't pass up an opportunity like that, Greg.* Those were his words. And you know what, she was with a friend, someone she was meant to be able to trust, someone who should have looked out for her. I tried to tell him that, but . . . I don't want to drag him through the mud here, but he said some pretty vile things, about what he'd done, about Lucy, about all of us."

"So he was angry?"

"No, not at all. Seriously, I don't think I ever saw him angry. It was worse in a way—he was dismissive, laughing about it, belittling her, as if nothing else mattered except his own enjoyment, getting what he wanted. I mentioned the Piranesi and he uttered some expletive or other and turned his back on me, started to walk away. That made me *so* angry. The arrogance of it. I grabbed hold of him, pulled him around—so yeah, it was me who ripped the buttons from his shirt. He pushed me away, but I could see he was thrown off balance by it . . ." Greg looked out across the garden and stared for a few seconds in silence, as if picturing the scene. "I've been back to that area since, in the summer, and it was a surprise to see how rocky the slopes are. With the snow it looked smooth—steep, but smooth. I pushed him. In my head, I imagined him tumbling backward down the slope, having to crawl back up, kind of like a humiliation, and I wanted to see him humiliated. But I didn't realize there was a kind of ledge part of the way down, with a much steeper drop to the glacier. Couldn't believe it when I saw him disappear. And then I heard . . . even from there, I heard him land. He didn't cry out, didn't scream, but I heard him land."

"Did you . . . ?"

Foster wasn't even sure what the question was, but Greg nodded and said, "I got down as far as the ledge. I couldn't get down the rest of the way, but I could see him. I knew he was dead. I sat there for ten minutes, maybe more, and then it got too cold and I climbed up the slope and walked back a different way to the village. While I was walking I realized I couldn't admit to being there. Had I meant to kill him? No. Of course not. Would a court believe that? Maybe."

"You could've just said he'd fallen. At least they would have known where to look for the body."

Greg smiled sadly. "Don't you think I've thought about that many times over the years? I was in a mess. I'd just killed someone, Foster. A friend. I didn't mean to do it, but my behavior leading up to it just didn't look good. Besides, by the time I got back, I couldn't even remember where it had happened. I told you I went back once during the summer, a few years later, and I did that in the hope it would remind me of the spot where it happened." He shook his head, expressing his failure to find that place again. "And that's all of it. That's the story."

"Not quite." Greg looked puzzled, and Foster said, "It's not quite the whole story. Something I discovered only this morning. You gamed the art market to ensure I became a success."

Clearly impressed, Greg said, "How did you find out?"

"Hamer, a former Kroll guy in New York."

"Heard of him. I should start using him myself." He nodded. "You're a hugely talented artist, Foster. I gave you an early boost, that's all, got the ball rolling."

"The world's full of talented artists no one's heard of. Don't get me wrong, I'm grateful for everything I have, for the freedom I have to paint, but it's pretty weird to know that you essentially manufactured my success because you felt guilty about killing my father."

"*That* isn't why I did it." Greg looked confounded by the assumption, and stared at him for a few seconds before continuing. "Foster, I didn't do those things because I killed Charlie or because I . . . I don't know, felt responsible for your existence or anything like that. I did it because I loved your mother. Totally. It broke my heart when she died. You have to know how much I tried to help her. I tried so hard, but I couldn't, and it wasn't enough. So I helped you instead. That's all there was to it."

"But . . ." No one had suggested there was anything between Greg and Lucy. It would explain why he'd been so incensed by Charlie's behavior, but it sat oddly with the story. Unless, of course, that too had been Greg's secret. "Did she know you were in love with her?"

"Yeah, she knew." He sounded more despondent, more haunted, than he had as he'd recounted the story about killing Charlie. "Marianne and Lucy had already been in Italy three months before the rest of us arrived. They'd already become firm friends. I arrived and there was no question, Lucy and I fell for each other at first sight, but it never came to anything—a couple of late-night kisses, nothing more—because Lucy didn't want to betray her friend. See, for those three months, Marianne had talked non-stop about this boy from home who was coming out to Bologna and how much she liked him. I respected Lucy for acting like that, but it killed us both—sorry, awkward choice of words." Foster didn't say anything, too busy trying to assimilate all this information, and Greg continued, saying, "She wrote to me, over a year later, saying it was the biggest mistake of her life—that in trying to avoid upsetting Marianne, she'd made the two of us so unhappy. And she said it was too late, which it wasn't, not for me. But I was in San Francisco when the letter arrived, didn't even see it for another month, and by the time I did see it, she was already dead. I wasn't to know it, but that letter was pretty much her suicide note. I'm sorry, I really do feel I shouldn't be talking to you about these things."

"It's okay. I mean, it's a lot to take in, but it's okay."

Greg looked simultaneously broken and relieved.

"You're the first person I've told most of this, and I know you could wreck my life with it if you wanted to, but I'm still glad I told you. I think I've been waiting to tell someone for the last thirty years."

"I'm glad, too." There was still too much to think about, but one phrase that Greg had used suddenly popped back into Foster's head and he said, "What did you mean by feeling responsible for my existence?" Greg looked confused and Foster added, "You said you didn't help me because you killed Charlie or felt responsible for my existence, something like that."

Greg stared at him in shock for a few long moments. "Oh God." He looked ready to reach for his wine glass, but saw it was empty and drank some water instead. "Foster, I really . . . Look, there's no easy way to tell you this. Lucy went back to England for an abortion. When Charlie disappeared she couldn't go through with it. I think that played a big part in her breakdown."

Foster took in what he was saying, then laughed, and couldn't even understand why he laughed. He leaned back and put his hands behind his head.

Greg had obviously been expecting a dramatic response, but not this one. "You find this funny?"

Foster lowered his hands again and said, "I only exist because you killed my father. You've got to admit, that's pretty Shakespearean stuff."

Greg laughed too, just once, then looked ashamed of himself, saying, "I see what you mean. It probably does all seem a little Prince of Denmark if you weren't directly involved at the time. But . . . Foster, I'm truly sorry about what happened with your dad, and I've relived it a million times, wishing it could have ended differently, but even so, losing Lucy was without question the defining event of my entire life. I don't think I've ever totally gotten over it."

Foster could see it, in his face, in his eyes. He looked so ingrained with that loss that Foster could easily believe it had weighed more heavily upon him than the accidental killing of his friend.

"I always resented her." Greg looked puzzled, and Foster said, "She chose to abandon me, and I know that isn't fair, I know no one really chooses to kill themselves, but when you're a kid it's hard to see it that way."

"She had a complete breakdown after you were born." Greg shook his head, struggling with the memory. "But she was the most beautiful person, just more fragile than any of us knew. And it's true what Marianne told you—yes, I heard all about your visit—you look like Charlie, but you have Lucy's soul."

"Thanks, I guess. And thanks for being so candid with me. It'll probably take a while for all of this to sink in, but I'm grateful for hearing it."

"I'm glad. And I'm sorry."

"For killing my dad or saving me?"

Greg opened his mouth, ready to respond, then realized Foster was joking, and he smiled a little. It seemed then as if another weight had been lifted, with the realization that Greg's story would never have the same gravitational pull on Foster that it exerted on him. Foster had been born with the tragic elements of this story within him, and carried them as easily as he carried his own being. He had never known either parent, and no number of stories would ever replace that missing bond.

Yet later, as Foster headed back across the lagoon in the launch, he kept thinking of his mother. It was strange that, in disappearing, Charlie had inadvertently ensured the story would always be about him, rather than about his victim. And later, in those early biographical sketches of Foster, she would once again be consigned to the lowly position of footnote in the artist's tragic story.

How could it be, he wondered, that someone who had been so loved could have disappeared so completely? And how could he, of all people, have helped conspire to erase her from this, her own story?

I fear for him daily. What an inheritance! And what can I possibly offer him to make his life as it should be? I'm so sorry, G, I've done everything wrong, and can think of few ways to make any of it right again. I ask you only to remember, if you must remember anything of me, that he was my child, too. Think of that sometimes, and perhaps of how we might have been happy, had I not made such a terrible mess of things. Forever, L.

Thirty-Five

Foster buried himself in the studio as soon as they got back to Berlin. Daniela returned to her apartment in Kreuzberg, but came back at the weekend, melding seamlessly with his obsessive working hours.

On Saturday night he worked on the glacier painting until tiredness got the better of him. And even then he collapsed onto the paint-covered couch and lay on his side, looking across the studio, trying to decide if it was finished or if some more work might still improve it.

He fell asleep there and woke the next morning to the smell of coffee. In a mirror image of another occasion a few weeks earlier, Daniela was sitting on the floor in front of the couch, watching him sleep.

She smiled. "You look like a little boy when you sleep."

"Is that a good thing?"

She kissed him and held up the mug of coffee she'd brought him. He sat up, took the coffee, and sipped at it, the aroma reviving him as much as the taste.

Daniela said, "You finally added a figure to the glacier painting."

"Yes." He glanced at it even as he answered, and was happy with it, for now at least.

"It's a woman."

"Yes."

"I hadn't expected that, but it's beautiful. I think it'll be the highlight of the show."

Mention of the show only reminded him of the Comic Sans letters, four more of which had arrived while they'd been in Venice.

"Speaking of the opening, I thought I'd invite Polly and her husband, maybe some of the other guys from The New Painters."

"That's a good idea."

"And Gagosian were talking to Claudia about doing a retrospective look at the whole group. They want to know if I'll be involved."

"And will you?"

"I guess it's the least I can do."

She smiled. "That's also good."

"It probably won't stop them hating me."

"No, but it's a start."

She climbed up onto the couch next to him.

"You'll get paint on you."

"I don't mind."

And she put her hand across his stomach, radiating warmth through him, restoring him, and the two of them sat like that, looking across at the vast glacial expanse, and the small female figure trapped within it, waiting to be found.

Acknowledgments

I have a lot of people to thank for their help in the planning and publication of this book. Firstly, as ever, I'm indebted to my agent, Deborah Schneider, and the rest of the team at Gelfman Schneider/ICM Partners. I also want to thank the excellent team at Thomas & Mercer, particularly Laura Deacon, Jack Butler, Ian Pindar, and Gemma Wain.

Professor Christian Jackowski, the director of the Institut für Rechtsmedizin at the University of Bern in Switzerland, offered invaluable advice, and I hope he'll forgive me for any license I've shown in the description of my fictional institute. Equally helpful were Christian Eckert and his staff at the wonderful Omnia Mountain Lodge in Zermatt, who helped me get up close and personal with glaciers. And given all the assistance they've afforded me over the years, I'm delighted to finally repay my Venetian home from home, the Ca' Sagredo, with a walk-on part in one of my books.

And finally, thanks to the morning crew at MJ's, for keeping me both grounded and more or less in one piece. With particular thanks to Rob Cormack for loaning me "that line"!

About the Author

Kevin Wignall is a British writer, born in Brussels in 1967. He spent many years as an army child in different parts of Europe and went on to study politics and international relations at Lancaster University. He became a full-time writer after the publication of his first book, *People Die* (2001). His other novels are *Among the Dead* (2002); *Who is Conrad Hirst?* (2007), shortlisted for the Edgar Award and the Barry Award; *Dark Flag* (2010); *The Hunter's Prayer* (2015, originally titled *For the Dogs* in the USA), which was made into a film directed by Jonathan Mostow and starring Sam Worthington and Odeya Rush; *A Death in Sweden* (2016); *The Traitor's Story* (2016); *A Fragile Thing* (2017); *To Die in Vienna* (2018); *When We Were Lost* (2019); and *The Names of the Dead* (2020).